Lost Cause

Life Sucks #8

Elise Faber

Lost Cause
by Elise Faber
Newsletter sign-up

LOST CAUSE
Copyright © 2023 ELISE FABER
Print ISBN: 978-1-63749-112-6
eBook ISBN: 978-1-63749-111-9

LIFE SUCKS SERIES

Life Sucks Series
Train Wreck
Hot Mess
Dumpster Fire
Clusterf*@k
FUBAR
Perfect Storm
Free Fall
Lost Cause

ONE

LEX

S quinting against the blackness, I adjusted the toggle on
my goggles.

Adjusted the settings so I could see more clearly.

Could see the woman who'd just gotten up, who would
soon descend the stairs from the apartment above her shop and
get ready for the day.

She wasn't the owner of Darlington's bakery, but she started
working at the same early hour.

When the sun wasn't up.

Hell, it wasn't even peeking over the horizon in the distance
yet.

Pitch black.

But *I* could see her, could see every inch of her gorgeous
body—from that lush ass to those tits that made a man hard, to
her face, pretty in a delicate way. I couldn't see the freckles
dusting the bridge of her nose and cheeks or the bright copper of
her hair—my night vision goggles saw in shades of green and

black—or blue to orange to red if I switched on thermal imaging.

But I'd memorized the pattern of them anyway.

Tonight, I stuck with the classic green as I watched her move through her apartment, catching glimpses of her through the windows as she got dressed and pulled her hair into a messy ponytail and then moved into her kitchen.

Here, she switched on the under-cabinet lights, so I adjusted too.

Back to normal view, zooming in, focusing on the brand of tea she was drinking today.

Filing it away with the other bits of information I'd learned about Francesca Lyon—Lee-own, not Lie-on—since I'd first picked up her file.

It had joined a plethora of others on the Lyons.

The only difference was that it was thin.

I'd thought it meant that she was better at covering her tracks.

Now, though, I wasn't so sure.

Francesca—Frankie—didn't live like a woman hiding from her past.

She had roots here—a business, friends, a surrogate family. One I knew well, considering that Carter and Chance Jackson and I had practically been the Three Musketeers growing up. The Jacksons were solid, good judges of character. Mostly because they had two former FBI agents in their family—and one current now that I was back in proximity to them.

Because that was one thing I'd never doubted.

They may not be blood, but DNA didn't limit who the Jacksons viewed as theirs.

I was theirs.

And...so was Frankie.

But she wasn't what she pretended to be.

I knew it from that case file, from the stack of folders that went with it.

So, I watched as she made her tea, watched as she tugged on a sweatshirt, flicked off the light, and changed to night vision as she exited through her apartment door, shifted to the shop windows as she descended the interior staircase, waited until she reappeared downstairs.

Lights on.

Binoculars switching modes again.

And then ice speared right through my heart.

Ice filled my veins, my cells.

Ice had me *moving*—pounding down the stairs from the apartment I'd leased, the one that was located over Carter's and Chance's PI firm, the one with its own interior staircase, so I knew the exact layout of Frankie's space.

Fifteen steps down.

Thirty of my long paces across Carter and Chance's office.

Forty to clear the sidewalk on this side, the road, the sidewalk on the other.

Three to the front door.

One booted foot connecting with the lock on the plate glass door.

It exploded inward, causing the two people inside, one looking pale and shocked, the other ice cold with a gun in hand, to spin toward me.

"FBI," I commanded. "Drop the gun and get on the ground!"

"Lex," Frankie began, hand clamped to her chest, but recovered enough to speak. "This is my—"

I knew exactly who the man was.

This man was why I was here in Darlington in the first place.

I'd hoped—

Well, it didn't fucking matter what I'd hoped.

Francesca Lyon was in front of me, interacting with a known member of a crime conglomerate.

"Get on the ground," I ground out.

Francis Lyon—Frankie's father—looked at me, sighed, and set the gun on the floor. He kicked it away and laid down, folding his hands behind his head in a practiced motion.

Because he'd been arrested before.

Many times over.

Only the charges never stuck.

This time they would.

I'd make certain of it.

I looked back to the curvy, redhead who'd almost had me fooled. "You too, Frankie."

She blinked, paling further. "What?"

"Get on the ground and lace your hands behind your head."

Two

The slam of the heavy metal door made me jump.

But this time I didn't jerk my gaze up, didn't look hopefully toward the exit of the cell, hoping that this was all a mistake, a stupid misunderstanding, that I wasn't actually currently sitting in a jail cell.

Having been arrested by the most beautiful man I'd ever met.

Icy blue eyes. Dark, scruffy beard. Big, built body that could shelter a woman, could keep her safe...

From exactly this situation.

But he'd put me there. Left me. And...

I didn't know what was happening.

I hadn't seen my father in going on five years.

But I'd hardly seen him before then—not unless it was for him to lecture me about some mistake I'd made or the five pounds I'd gained or the fact that I wasn't dressing in a lady-like enough fashion.

Only, he'd said it in not nice terms.

Very not nice terms.

So, I'd left.

And because he hadn't often thought about me even *when* I'd lived under his roof, and then I'd been out of sight, so he *wouldn't* think about me...five years had passed before he'd darkened my door.

For what, I didn't know.

We hadn't even got beyond the sour expression on his face as he'd looked around Earthly Delights, the shop I'd worked my ass off to make great—on my own—before Lex was bursting in through the front door like a freaking action hero.

I'd thought—

My eyes closed, tears stinging the backs of my lids.

I'd thought he'd somehow been walking by, seen me taken by surprise, and had rushed in to rescue me.

But instead...

I'd ended up in handcuffs.

Dragged from my shop with the metal brackets pushing into my skin, a handful of local residents looking on. It must have been hard to *not* be attracted to the flashing lights, the sirens, the sight of one of their own—something I'd worked really hard to become—being hauled away in cuffs.

I got it.

I really did.

I just...

It was awful, and my dad was a jerk who lived in 1952, but he was still my dad and he couldn't be involved in—

He had a gun.

I swallowed, my eyes burning more, tears threatening to spill over.

My dad had a gun and Lex had known exactly who he was and—

"Ms. Lyon."

I jerked again, but this time my head *did* lift, not having realized an officer had come into the cell I was being held in, not realizing she'd come close, was crouching a couple of feet away from where I was sitting crammed in the corner where the small metal bench met the wall.

Straightening, I dashed the back of my hand across my eyes. "I'm sorry. I didn't realize..." I shrugged, blew out a quiet breath. "Did you need something?"

The woman wore a deep blue button down that contrasted with her dark brown eyes. Her hair was pulled into a tight, slicked-back ponytail, a riot of brown curls escaping at the back of her head. Her black slacks were crisp and fell perfectly to the tops of her shoes.

And she was studying me closely.

Very closely.

Then she straightened out of the crouch, eyes not leaving mine as she announced, "You're free to go."

I blinked.

"I—" My lips pressed flat, released. "But how?" I asked softly, everything I knew about police procedure coming from the fact that I watched cop shows on TV with near obsession. I hadn't had my one phone call or anything.

And what about bail?

Wait, did I have to have charges for that?

Wait, *did* I have charges?

I hadn't even been interviewed beyond a few questions at the shop.

And I'd been sitting in this cell for *hours*.

"Your father's attorney made a very compelling case for you to be released," she said softly.

My eyes went wide. "My father has an attorney—" I shook my head because, of course, he did. "He owns a lot of businesses," I whispered mostly to myself, "and he's always busy but—"

Clarity struck me. "Is this some tax thing? Like his accountant messed up or he tried to get out of paying or..."

I trailed off, mostly because the other woman's expression of pure disbelief had my words stoppering up in the back of my throat.

Then her expression cleared, and she seemed to shake herself. "I believe Mr. Henderson—your father's *criminal defense* attorney—"

My heart sank to my shoes.

"—is waiting with a car out front."

"Oh," I whispered.

She studied me again, long and deep and—I felt my eyes start to burn again.

"Right," I whispered. "So, I'll just—" I pointed at the open cell door.

She nodded, stepped back, and waved a hand for me to proceed her.

Then came the very awkward process of retrieving my belongings—my smart watch, my bracelet and earrings, the small drawing that Cole, the son one of my close friends, Kim, had drawn for me. It was adorable—a picture of the two of us playing choo-choos from the train-obsessed kiddo, all squiggly lines and colors outside the lines and—

It meant something.

And I didn't like the way that the woman unfolded it, staring at it for a long time before carefully folding it back up and handing it to me.

I tucked it into my back pocket, where I often kept it when I was feeling alone.

Trying to remind myself that I wasn't.

Because I *wasn't*.

"I'll walk you out," the woman said after another long moment.

"Thanks...um...officer—"

"Agent Phillips," she replied with a smile that lit up her face. "Or, unfortunately, since my parents are history buffs, Athena."

My eyes went a little wide, but I nodded. "That fits." And it did—tall, strong, beautiful.

Totally lived up to that goddess name.

A tilt of her head, those curls bouncing.

And then she waved her arm again, indicating that I move toward the exit, that I walk in front of her again. "Agent Phillips," I said softly. "Does that mean you work for the FBI too?"

A pause, long enough that we'd mostly woven our way through the entirety of desks at the police station.

"Ms. Lyon."

I stopped, glanced back. "Yeah?"

"Never mind." She started walking again, and this time I trailed her, luckily closely enough that I didn't miss it when she said, "I'm Lex's partner."

I inhaled sharply.

Lex who'd stared at me with frosty eyes.

Who'd snapped cold cuffs on my wrists.

Who'd clipped out sharp, frigid commands.

"Oh," I whispered. "I see."

And I did.

Because we'd pushed through the door and out into the lobby and I finally processed that we weren't inside Darlington's police station—though, in fairness, it wasn't like I'd spent any amount of time in the home of the Darlington PD.

But we weren't in a small town's police headquarters.

We were in an FBI field office, the crest inlaid right there on the tile floor, the bronze letters secured to the wall.

Athena—Agent Phillips—glanced down at me, doing more studying. I felt her gaze remain on me even as I broke away, searching the space for a criminal defense attorney.

The lobby was busy and there were plenty of smarmy, suit-wearing men taking up space.

So, it wasn't easy.

"He's in the blue tie," Athena murmured, making me jump again because the voice came from very close to my ear.

"Right," I whispered. "Is—" Then I clamped my teeth together.

Because I'd been about to ask if it was safe to go with him.

"What?" Her expression and tone were curious.

"I—"

"Ms. Lyon." The cold voice made me shiver and step back, almost bumping into Agent Phillips. "I have a driver available to take you home."

"No, thank you," I said, reaching into my pocket and pulling out my phone. "I'll get my own ride home."

"That's not—"

I didn't know this man.

I *did* know that everything about him screamed that I didn't want to.

Luckily, I also knew how to deal with men like this.

Because I'd grown up with them.

So, I ignored him, spun around to thank Agent Phillips, and then walked to the reception desk, standing there while I ordered my car from the rideshare app, while I waited for it to show up, not responding to any of his questions or commands and remaining near enough to those agents behind the desk that he wouldn't feel comfortable enough—or be dumb enough—to manhandle me outside.

And then when the Lyft showed after he'd walked off in a huff, I asked an agent to escort me to it.

Good thing I did.

Because he was still there, smoke all but coming out of his ears as he stood, arms crossed, outside a black SUV.

I continued ignoring, thanked the agent, and got in the car.

We drove off and I didn't miss that Agent Phillips was standing on the sidewalk, watching me go.

Just like I didn't miss that the SUV followed me all the way home.

THREE

Athena leaned back against the wall of my office, ankles crossed, folder in her hands, flipping through the pages one after one.

Slowly.

Deliberately.

And we'd worked together long enough that I knew exactly what emotion she was trying to convey with that page flipping.

Disapproval.

I sighed, pushed my chair back from my desk, propping my feet on the corner of the dark wooden top—that corner being the single small portion that wasn't covered in more folders or computer paraphernalia.

"Spill it, Attie."

She scowled, closed the folder, and strode to the chair on the other side of my desk, reaching over the top of it to shove my feet off.

They landed with a *thunk*, sending my body jerking.

I *could* have stopped them...but that would have prevented me from sending her a wounded look.

Which she promptly brushed off.

"First, that's disgusting," she said, nodding at my feet. "Do you *know* what's on the bottom of your shoes?"

I shrugged. "I'm just building my immune system."

"And mine," she muttered, holding up the folder that I'd passed her just a few minutes before. She reached for the bottle of sanitizer in the opposite corner of my desk—one she'd stashed there after she'd realized my penchant for boot-propping—then sat back, rubbing a glob between her hands.

"Second?" I prompted, knowing that she had a tendency to list, and that the listing sure as fuck didn't stop at *one.*

"And *second*," she muttered, "I hate that nickname, as you well know."

"I know." A beat. "Attie."

Her eyes narrowed. "Third, I'll quit my fucking job if Frankie Lyon has anything to do with her father's criminal activities."

I bit back a sigh, knew we were getting right into it. "She springs from a poisoned well, Ats."

Since that was a designated acceptable nickname, she didn't comment on it. Instead, she pulled her legs up beneath her—not worried about germs from her shoes in that position, apparently (and cue me rolling my eyes)—and began ticking off on her fingers as she said, "Her finances don't show any proof of a woman hiding anything. She lives small. Her car is used. Her clothes aren't designer. She works long hours in that shop of hers, and even longer ones in the extra classes she puts on. For free." A pointed look in my direction. "She even delivers home-made meals to seniors for fuck's sake."

"Francis Lyon funded that same shop she cooks her meals in."

Attie's brows lifted. "From a trust fund that Frankie had—

one of the *few* things she had. And a trust fund that she hasn't touched since."

All of this was true.

All of *this* was why she'd almost had me fooled.

If she hadn't been clandestinely meeting her crime boss of a father before dawn, I might have gone on believing it.

"Let me ask you something," Attie said after a long moment.

I braced. "Go ahead."

"Did you find anything to prove a connection between Frankie and her father in her apartment? In her store?"

I sighed.

Because she already knew the answer to that, knew exactly the same thing I did.

That I'd found jack shit.

"Your past is impacting your present," she said quietly. Not gently. Gentle wasn't Attie. Gentle was...

Frankie.

Except, that was bullshit.

Case in point, I had to put her in cuffs that morning.

But did I?

"You got fucked over by Hailey—"

Christ.

"*Don't.*"

Her eyes narrowed and—proving she wasn't gentle—she pushed right on. "Hailey fucked you over. You didn't see it. *I* didn't see it. No one did. But just because you were fucked over by a woman once doesn't mean that every other woman is out to get you, and it doesn't fucking mean that every other woman on this planet has that same evil streak."

"I know that," I snapped, shoving out of my chair and grabbing my jacket.

It was late and it had been a long fucking day and—

I was done.

"Do you?" she asked, head turning to follow me, long, lean

body unfolding from my chair. She grabbed her own jacket, and we'd worked together long enough that I knew exactly what this signified too.

She intended to walk out with me to our cars.

Christ.

"I know it, Attie."

Her mouth pursed, but she didn't comment on the nickname this time, just shrugged into her coat and followed me into the hall.

"I'm just saying—"

"Drop it, okay?" I snapped. "It's been a long enough day without you riding my ass about shit that's not going to change."

Silence as we walked to the elevators.

I jabbed the button, glanced over at her. Her lips were pressed flat, eyes on her phone she'd pulled out of her pocket, scrolling through an email by the look of it.

The elevator dinged, and we shoved onto the already full car.

Releasing a silent—but relieved because she was going to listen for once—breath, I crammed myself to the side. I was a big guy and took up more than my fair share of space—not something I was uncomfortable with because it wasn't like I could just make myself smaller, but it was also a fact of life that I was aware of, so I tried to not be an asshole about it.

Attie took the other side.

Another message.

But one I was ignoring because the elevator was full and it had been a fucking long day and—

My phone buzzed in my pocket.

I managed to extract it without elbowing anyone in the face, brought it up—

Just as the elevator doors opened and people got off, others got on. This meant I had to cram myself further to the side, further into the corner, and it took a few seconds for me to get it up to my face. By which time several more texts came through.

There was only one message chain that went a flurry a minute, setting my goddamned pants off like they were hiding a vibrator.

The Jackson Family chain.

They must have heard.

Frankly, it was a fucking surprise they hadn't heard before then, that they hadn't been blowing up my phone all day.

As I unlocked my screen and began scrolling through the texts, seeing the shock, the anger, the demands for me to explain myself, I knew I'd likely fucked my relationship with them.

I didn't bother to reply, just swiped and jabbed at the screen so notifications for that chain would be turned off until I decided to turn them back on—which would probably not be until the next fucking century.

Because Frankie was on the chain.

Because I was getting too close to this investigation and I knew it.

Because sooner or later, I would need to step back, let the rest of the team take over.

But I wanted Francis Lyon to pay, and I wanted him to pay big.

So...just a little while more.

And then Lyon would be in jail permanently, would stop fucking up innocent people's lives, would stop fucking with *my* life.

It would all work out, all be straightened out.

They would see.

They would understand why they could never, ever trust Frankie Lyon.

Not ever again.

Four

Thankfully, the black SUV housing my father's lawyer—his *criminal defense* lawyer—kept driving once the Lyft had pulled up to the back side of Earthly Delights.

I got out, extended my thanks, then walked through the shadow-filled alleyway to reach the front door.

And froze.

Because...

A crash.

Lex's booted foot slamming into the door before he'd burst through it like it was tissue paper. Then he'd emerged like a fucking action hero, charging toward the center of the shop, the large table where I housed the freshly made treats for my customers.

Homemade granola that always sold out, brownies that were both reasonably healthy and to die for, kale chips, breakfast bars, protein cookies—

Anything I could think of that would be tasty and filled with good stuff.

I didn't just run a health store—though vitamins and supplements were a good chunk of my stock—I also focused on natural cleaning products (that wouldn't break the bank and actually worked), the aforementioned homemade goodies and cooking classes so my customers could make them on their own, cruelty free makeup without scary additives, and I even had a program of renting glass jars and had bulk bins of things like flour (unbleached), rolled oats, cane sugar, and snacks ranging from pretzels to unpopped rainbow corn kernels to seeds and quinoa and—

Well, a lot of things.

Food had once been my enemy.

My biggest, greatest, my most dangerous enemy.

But now...it was my joy.

And I loved helping other people find it too.

I moved to the front door, pushed it forward, expecting it to just open—considering Lex's action star antics early that morning—frowning when it didn't. "What the—?"

I looked down, and my heart squeezed once. *Hard.*

It had been boarded up—or a board had been attached to the door frame and below the broken handle that Lex had kicked in. Metal hardware had been screwed into it, and the entire thing was secured with a padlock.

Likely, this had been done by my friend's brother, Rob.

He was a contractor by trade and a nice person and—

My eyes burned for the umpteenth time that day.

My friends knew how important my store was to me, so they'd made sure it was safe.

But also...

That meant they knew I'd been hauled off in handcuffs.

And *that* was...worse.

Dashing a hand across my cheeks, the burning having turned to tears—also for the umpteenth time that day—I moved around to the back of my apartment, fishing my keys from my pocket but pausing before I actually inserted them into the lock.

Because there was a note tacked to the door.

Call me to let me know you're okay.
Rob will come over in the morning with parts
to fix the door.
    —M

Shit, I was leaking again.

Tears streaking down my cheeks, leaving hot, wet tracks in their wake.

I didn't bother brushing them aside, not this time.

I just pushed the keys into the lock, wrestled with it, and shoved the door open. Then I leaned back against it and breathed, wondering where it had all gone so wrong, wondering about the little Agent Phillips had said.

Wondering if everything I'd thought I'd known was a lie.

And knowing it probably was.

"Enough," I whispered.

And then I walked through the narrow hall that split off into two short corridors with doors at their ends. Both were open, when they would normally be closed, hiding the respective spaces behind them. One the staircase that led up to my apartment, the other my mess of a stockroom, crammed with a seemingly never-ending parade of boxes I needed to sort through.

Funny how just that morning I'd been thinking about needing to hire a couple of high school kids to help out with that, and now...

I wanted to turn to the right, walk up the stairs to my apartment, and forget that today had ever happened.

My feet took me to the left anyway.

Down the dim hall, past the kitchen, past the entrance to the front of Earthly Delights, and through the doorway.

Flicking on the lights in the storeroom, and...

Revealing an utter fucking mess.

It looked like a bear had torn through the space. Boxes were ripped open, their contents dumped on the floor. My shelves were pulled away from the wall, anchors forced from the sheetrock, leaving an array of holes behind.

There were others too.

Larger holes where the walls had been opened, clear down to the studs.

Shock had stuck me in place as I took in the devastation around me.

But then I was moving again, kicking through the detritus, suddenly panicked because if the storeroom looked like this then what had happened to the front room, to my bulk bins and carefully crafted displays of cleaning products, to my granola and brownies and—

I burst out from behind the register and skidded to a stop, the deep punch to my gut, the knife stuck into my belly nearly taking me to my knees.

My fingers bit into the wooden counter.

I wavered and my vision darkened at the edges.

Then...I slowly sank down into a crouch, hands going to my hair, forehead pressing to my knees. "No," I whispered.

Please let it be a dream.

A nightmare.

A—

My eyes caught on the carefully organized shelves that were behind the counter—on what *had been* the carefully organized shelves. Now the baskets were overturned, their contents spread out on the tile floor, the labels and bags and tiny hemp ribbon bows I'd spent hours tying.

Until my fingers had cramped.

Until I'd wanted to launch them out the window.

Until I'd perfected them and they were one of *my* things, one of those special touches that made Earthly Delights, Earthly Delights.

That was when the tears came again—but they weren't mopey, weren't woe-is-me. They were *fucking furious*.

Angry tears that dripped down my cheeks and onto my shirt, soaking into the collar.

I pushed to my feet, saw my table display was destroyed, my bulk bins scooped through. Everything inside them would need to be thrown away. I couldn't be sure they hadn't been contaminated, that they wouldn't now make someone sick.

Bottles were scattered everywhere. More boxes were torn open, products ruined.

More waste.

More of my hard work stomped on.

So no, I wasn't sad.

I was still crying, but I was *pissed*—at the people who'd stomped on my life, wearing big, ugly boots that left dirty prints on my floor.

At the man who'd put a similar boot through my front door.

And ruined everything I'd worked for.

Fuck Lex Blackwell.

I would never—*ever*—forgive him for this.

Knowing that, vowing that, I allowed the tears to flow, and then I moved around the counter...

And I started cleaning.

FIVE

LEX

She'd been at it for hours.

I don't know why I'd gone back to my apartment—still ignoring the text chain, which was nearing a hundred unread messages—and immediately picked up my binoculars.

Maybe it was habit.

Maybe it was the case.

Maybe it was that I just needed to see her.

The last was something else I ignored, and it was as heavy as the weight of my cell with all those messages in my pocket.

I exhaled, and fiddled slightly with the controls on my binoculars, focusing in on her as she slowly and methodically emptied the large bins of grains—one scoopful at a time, bend and scoop, lift and drop it into the large gray trashcan I'd watched her drag in, watched her line with a black bag.

Lift. Scoop. Dump.

Rinse. Repeat.

Until she stopped, dropped the scoop onto the counter, and returned to the can, pulling the bag out with a heave.

Her body wavered, the bulging bag nearly taking her down as she tossed it over her shoulder.

Then she staggered toward the door in the back.

I moved, shifting my focus there, knowing she would push out, kick a rock in place so it would stay open and she wouldn't get locked out, and then she'd proceed to the dumpster, where it would take at least three heaves to get it up and into the metal container.

That accomplished, I expected her to go back to scooping, or clearing off the large tables that normally housed her homemade granola—that I'd had for breakfast every single morning since I'd moved back to Darlington—or even reorganizing the shelves.

But she didn't.

She moved to the counter, picked up something and shoved it in her pocket then went back out that door, kicking the rock out of the way so it shut, and then moved through the shadowed alley and down Darlington's main street.

And out of sight.

My stomach clenched.

It wasn't safe to be out in the middle of the night. Even if Darlington was the quote-unquote perfect Hallmark town, it was dark and late and she was a woman walking unprotected by herself—

No.

That wasn't why I was worried.

She was a suspect.

Or not—since we hadn't found anything to charge her on and we'd released her.

She was the daughter of a criminal, had that criminal in her store.

Colluding.

Definitely.

Involved.

Likely.

That was why I dropped my binoculars onto my desk, why I shoved my feet into my boots, grabbed my holster, my jacket, and exited my apartment—this time through the back staircase, the cool ocean air hitting me, the hint of salt in it leaving my skin feeling sticky.

Loved the ocean.

Hated that.

Loved the beach.

Hated the sand in my shoes, the way it permeated straight through every layer of protection. It brought back memories of another time—of blistering days in a desert, fighting a war I didn't believe in.

Bare feet. Fine.

In my boots, the sand abrading at the soles of my feet, rubbing me raw between my toes, making each step heavier than the last.

Yeah, no.

Really fucking didn't like that.

But I didn't have time to focus on it.

I'd gone out the back, cutting off a block of distance I needed to travel, but she was still ahead of me. I moved quickly but silently, my boots making the barest whisper of sound on the sidewalk. I saw her hurrying forward in the distance, head down, shoulders hunched, and I had a memory of following after her another time, when I'd hurt her before.

Then with idiotic words and trying to be funny—but really, also fucking terrified because I liked her and couldn't like her, not with what I'd had to do.

I'd patched things up with her then.

I'd had to. For the case.

Now I didn't know why I followed her. She knew why I was in Darlington.

I didn't need to pretend anymore.

But...I still followed her down to the beach, in my fucking boots, sand pouring in, making each step heavier than the last.

I half expected her to be meeting someone, to be participating in some sort of illicit exchange.

I didn't expect to watch her sink onto the sand, legs seeming to give out, somehow ending up with them tucked beneath her and not snapping. I didn't expect to see her sit there, staring out at the darkness for a long, long time.

There was nothing to see—it wasn't particularly bright out, the moon hidden behind the clouds, the stars dim glimmers in the faraway sky. And even as my eyes gradually adjusted more and more to the darkness, there *still* wasn't much to take in.

The occasional white crest of a wave.

A faint silver glow from the moonlight above.

And a beautiful redhead sitting alone on a beach, staring out into nothing, looking fragile and breakable and—

It was a fucking act.

A deception.

For all I knew she was waiting for a boat to come in, preparing to help them unload a plethora of the drugs—or people—her father loved to peddle. Drugs and people that had paid for her upbringing, that had funded her shop, that had—

She moved, legs coming up, head resting on her knees.

Not bothering to stare out at nothing.

Not any longer.

Shoulders shaking.

Crying.

Something jabbed at my stomach, yanked up, leaving a wave of pain all through my torso...

And stopping at my heart.

In my heart.

I ignored it—because I was fucking good at that.

I pushed down the guilt—because I was fucking good at that too.

Then I strode forward, and dropped onto the sand behind her.

One leg on either side of her, not acknowledging her gasp of surprise as I whipped her around, forcing her to face me in the vee of my legs.

Tears, yup.

No, I didn't feel that.

I couldn't so...I *didn't*.

I couldn't so...I pulled the anger that was always smoldering in the pit of my stomach up...

And I let it fly.

Six

FRANKIE

One second, I was crying and promising it would be the last time I'd let myself do this—again.

And the next, a man had sat behind me, his legs surrounding me. Big hands whipped my body around.

Not a man.

Lex.

He opened his mouth and angry words came out. "What the fuck do you think you're doing?"

But I was angry too. Furious. More pissed than I'd ever been in my life.

Why did he have to look so fucking beautiful after what he'd done to me?

"Don't touch me!" I snapped, shoving at his hand.

"It's the middle of the night and you're out here alone, not even aware of your surroundings!"

He was right—which pissed me off even more.

As did the fact that he didn't stop touching me, hands clenching on my shoulders, face coming very close to mine.

As did that—mainly because this was one of my fantasies.

Not with the anger, with the fear and the tears, but sneaking out for a midnight picnic, sitting on the cool sand under the moonlight and stars, the warm frame of a man's—of *this* man's —body surrounding mine.

I'd feel safe and protected and wanted...just for being myself.

Not thinner, not prettier, not someone different.

Just me being seen and loved as *I* am.

But this man wasn't safe for me—I should have known the first time he'd been cruel, no matter the apology, no matter that he'd been nice since.

I should have known a man like him couldn't like me.

Not just *me*.

And worse, he was right. I wasn't being smart or safe.

Because I hadn't heard or sensed him come up behind me, not with the waves crashing on the shore, not with me so locked down into my own misery and tears.

Enough.

"Let go," I ground out, shoving against his chest, ignoring the hard planes there, the rugged muscles beneath my palms.

He didn't.

"Are you trying to get yourself killed?"

I flinched.

"Or raped? Or beat up? Your shit stolen?"

"This is Darlington," I began. "It's safe—"

"Bad shit happens in any town, baby. Perfect Hallmark expectations or not."

"I—" But I stopped, clamped my teeth together. Because he was right.

Because he'd called me *baby*.

He'd done that, used that endearment only once before...the night he'd been a dick and embarrassed me...and the night I'd forgiven him.

I wasn't going to do the same *this* night, even if the way that *baby* drifted down my skin, his deep, rasping voice sliding between my thighs, his warm body surrounding mine and—

"You're right," I said, jerking out of his hold and darting to my feet. Sand fluttered off my body, had filled my shoes, grinding between my toes, my shoes and socks. I should have worn flip-flops. "It was dumb to come here—a stupid risk—so, I'll just go home."

I turned for the dunes, for the path that led up between them, that would take me back downtown and to my trashed shop, to my small apartment, to the only place I'd ever felt at home...

A home that was in shambles.

I took exactly one step before I was hauled back against that strong chest, his arms wrapping around me, turning me to face him. He bent so our faces were very close, his eyes on mine, and I wondered what in the fuck-all he could see since it *was* the middle of the night.

But he saw something because he cursed under his breath, and then his fingers were wrapping around my wrist, and he was walking.

I was walking, having no choice but to keep up with his hurried steps.

Because it was either that or be dragged behind him.

He was big and strong, and his grip was like iron—I had no choice but to follow.

Follow him along the beach.

Follow him up between the dunes.

Follow him back to his apartment.

My lungs wheezed out all the air within them when he brought me to the exterior staircase and started up it. I had one at my store too, one that led up to a little balcony I'd filled with a chair, a table, and lots of plants, leaving barely enough room for my front door. It was tiny and cramped and only had a sliver of view of the ocean. But...it was mine.

Lex had a lot more.

He was on the right side of the street, could see more of the beach, looking over the row of single-story cottages that lined Darlington's beachfront.

Even now it was beautiful—an undulating stretch of dark navy and black, interspersed with dashes of white.

He dropped my hand, and I should have probably taken the chance to run.

But I was looking out at the ocean, wanting to be back on the stretch of beach, finding peace in the waves instead of crying on the shoreline.

And then I missed my opportunity—not that I held out much hope that I would have been able to avoid or outrun him if he wanted to stop me—as he wrapped his fingers around my wrist again and drew me inside.

We'd lived across the road from each other for almost a year.

But I'd never been inside his space.

And I don't know what I expected, but it wasn't *this*.

It was...empty.

Not exactly—there was a couch and a table, a TV. There was a microwave on the tiny kitchen's counter, a battered stool in front of it.

But no books, not a picture or plant. No pillows or a throw.

Empty.

Devoid.

Disquiet settled in my belly.

"What's that in your hand?"

The hemp bow roughly abraded my skin as I clenched my fist tighter, not wanting him to see, not wanting to open up further to this empty, devoid man who I'd thought I'd known but really had no fucking clue at all the person he was inside. Not wanting to admit that I'd been holding on to a fucking bow like I was clinging to the past...

Which I was.

I mean, my past wasn't all that great.

Most times it had been a nightmare.

Just...this was worse.

And maybe I was a glutton for punishment.

Because I let Lex peel back my fingers.

"What is this?" he asked, taking the bow.

"Nothing," I said quickly, trying to grab it back.

"Wait," he said, gaze going from mine, looking to the right.

I followed his stare, saw it...and my stomach convulsed. The man's apartment was a fucking wasteland...except for one thing, not revealed until he'd stepped back, until he'd turned to look at it.

An Earthly Delights bag sitting on the counter, kraft paper brown—

And attached to the handle...

Was one of my little bows.

I remembered carefully securing it a few days ago after picking out the perfect bow especially for him. I remembered taking extra time to make sure it sat just right on the hemp handle.

My eyes stung again, but I blinked back the tears.

No more tears.

I'd promised myself.

No more *fucking* tears.

No. More.

I turned my head away—

Fingers on my chin, turning it back. "What?"

It was a gentle question, as gentle as the hold on my face, gentle when a man as big and strong and *intense* as Lex *shouldn't* be able to be so soft, so sweet, so tender—

Except...it was all a lie.

I pulled back.

He wasn't any of those things. He wasn't gentle and tender and kind, not with me.

It was an act because he thought my father was...

What?

Worse than the bastard, shitty father I'd always thought he was, more than an asshole who'd controlled every bite that went in my mouth, every stitch of clothing, every haircut I'd had before I managed to find the strength to get out.

Some sort of monster who deserved to be arrested.

Some sort of monster who needed a criminal defense attorney.

Some sort of monster who mere association with meant I was equally as bad.

"What did he do?" I asked. "Agent Phillips said it wasn't tax-related."

A thunderstorm across a handsome face. "*Agent Phillips* needs to learn to keep her mouth shut."

"So it *is* some mistake with taxes?" My tone was hopeful, I knew it was.

But I couldn't help it.

I mean, it wasn't good, but it also...it also wasn't as bad, right? Just pay the taxes and be done with it. Fix the problem—

"It's not taxes."

My eyes flashed open, and I hadn't even realized they'd closed. "Then what is it?"

SEVEN

LEX

I stared at her.

Really studied every part of her face—the pert nose that called a man to kiss the tip of it, the smattering of freckles over the bridge, on her cheeks, the plump bottom lip that made me think of other plump pink lips...especially when her tongue darted out and left it glistening.

My cock got hard—a common problem when in her vicinity, but I ignored it.

Like always.

Because I was staring into her eyes, searching for any sign of deception.

And just like every other time I'd studied her over the last year, I didn't find a single bit of it.

Which meant I was either fucking terrible at my job, a fucking failure at reading people (something that had already been proven true before, unfortunately), or that she was telling the truth.

I knew what Agent Phillips—what Attie—would say.

She'd been Team Frankie from the moment we'd been positioned in this field office.

But I couldn't afford to be on her side.

Only...here in my apartment, the hideous fluorescent lights not hiding her face like the darkness at the beach, I had the sinking sensation that I was wrong again.

Just the other way around.

"You want to know?" I asked.

Her eyes flared. "Yes." Earnestness in her tone, her expression, those deep green irises.

Fuck they were pretty.

And I shouldn't even be having this conversation, I shouldn't have gone after her, shouldn't have brought her here, shouldn't—

"Drugs."

Another flare, but not with hope and curiosity.

Disbelief and hurt.

"No," she whispered. "That—"

"And women," I pressed. "Women and children."

She staggered back a step, that disbelief warring now with...horror.

Another blade to my gut, slicing up toward my heart.

"No," she whispered. "No, he can't—" Her eyes closed and she wavered, and for a second, I thought she'd go down, had actually moved toward her, intending to catch her before that happened. But then her eyes opened and she gasped when she saw me there, standing so close.

"He can," I said. "And he does. And you grew up in a house funded by their lives, their bodies, their—"

She gasped again, clamped a hand over her mouth like she was going to be sick, lurching backward, colliding with the arm of my couch.

She went down faster than I could reach her, knees cracking against the floor, palms slamming into the fake wood.

"Shit," I muttered, going to her, crouching down in front of her, reaching for her even though I shouldn't.

Really shouldn't.

"No," she whispered, and at first, I thought it was because she didn't want me to touch her.

But she didn't fight me when I sank back onto my ass, tugged her into my lap, held her close.

"No," she whispered again. "No, no, *no.*"

She froze and glanced up at me, eyes damp, but no tears escaping. "Tell me that there's a chance you're wrong," she said, still whispering.

"There is no chance, baby."

Her lids slid closed, one tear escaped, and she whispered, "Wh-what does he do with the kids?"

I stilled then stupidly lifted a hand, brushed the tear away, the dampness that ended up on my thumb burning like acid through my skin.

Her eyes opened again.

The churning in my gut swept all the way up to my heart.

I shouldn't have continued this conversation, shouldn't have given her more details about the case.

But I gave her this anyway. "You know."

A jerk.

Another eye-closing.

Then her head dropped, chin resting against her chest, sigh escaping. "How—" She clamped her lips closed, shook her head.

"What, baby?"

Baby.

I was a *fucking* idiot.

But it got those green eyes back on mine. "How could he do that?"

Not *it can't be true*.

Not hiding the shadows at the edges of her expression.

Not disguising her disgust.

Just...believing me.

"I don't know how anyone does that," I told her truthfully. "I don't know how anyone could exploit another person for their own gain, for money and power. I don't know how anyone could live with themselves when they make their living off the backs of others. But I also know"—I smoothed away another tear, rubbed it between thumb and forefinger—"that the type of people who do that are the people who I will *never* understand. They have an evil streak in them. It's burned onto their soul, sewn into the fiber of their being, and they will never hesitate to exploit a situation to get what they want."

She flinched.

And the fact that she didn't argue with me, that she accepted what I said, that she didn't stand up for her father circled right back into the forefront of my mind.

She believed me.

Some part of her believed me...

And that begged the question of *why*.

Why did she believe me so easily? Why had she left home? Why did she have no contact with her father in the year I'd been in Darlington...except for yesterday morning in her store.

When she'd walked downstairs and found him.

What had happened to her?

I opened my mouth to ask her, but she beat me to it, pushing against my chest so abruptly that I didn't react in time to keep her there, to keep her where I wanted.

Then she was on her feet.

"So all of this," she whispered, her hand moving between us, "all of the time we spent together, the relation—*friendship* I thought we were building..."

Her voice had dropped to a volume where I had to strain to hear it, and I put my feet under me, pushed up.

"...it was all about this? About my father?" She sucked in a breath, released it. "About the case you guys have been building?"

It was...

And it wasn't.

But I couldn't tell her that, couldn't expose the conflict in my belly, my mind, my heart.

I just...couldn't.

So, I said, "Yeah, baby. All of this, all of whatever *us* there is, was about your father." A beat. "About the case and my job and making sure justice is done."

"About my father," she repeated, almost absently.

Like that wasn't a surprise.

Like that...was how she'd lived her life.

Like...I had no fucking clue what she'd experienced.

The words shot out of me like bullets. But they were disjointed, flying wildly through the air. "Did he—" Her eyes came to mine. "Were you..." Stupid, so fucking stupid to be asking this. But I had to know if she'd been treated like the women, like the children her father traded in. "Were..."

"No," she whispered, gaze sliding away. "I was beyond privileged."

Why didn't I believe her?

"Frankie—"

"I hope you make him pay." A murmur.

I didn't know what to say to that, conflict had boiled up into the back of my throat, burning, stealing my ability to respond.

And I didn't get it back before she turned away from me.

Before I watched her walk to the front door, open it, and step through.

It wasn't until the door closed behind her that I realized the bow she'd been holding earlier, the bow that she'd been clinging to like it was the most precious object she'd ever come across was on the floor.

Left behind.

Alone.

Like her.

Eight

The sun coming in through the windows was the first thing I noticed when I peeled back my lids the next morning.

Mostly, because I was an early riser, because I didn't sleep much in general and I never had.

And *because* when I was up early, when I was busy, when I didn't sleep much the memories, the nightmares weren't able to crowd in.

But they had last night.

Crowding and shoving and cutting and—

A booted foot through my front door.

Handcuffs on my wrists.

Sneaking out in the middle of the night when I'd finally gotten the courage to leave.

Realizing that no one was coming after me.

Because they didn't care.

Pins jabbing into my scalp.

Being so damned hungry but unable to eat, because if I did—

Knock. Knock. Knock.

It wasn't a gentle announcement that someone was at my front door. It was a pounding, and it made me gasp. Though—thankfully—it made the memories closing in snap away, retreat back into the dark, dark recesses of my mind.

The knocking paused and then started up again, a steady pounding that was impossible to ignore.

It was also why I knew it couldn't be Rob, my friend Misty's brother.

He wouldn't pound, first of all, and he wouldn't continue doing it, sending waves of vibration up through the walls.

And he sure as hell wouldn't be doing it at the exterior door of my apartment.

He'd call or have Misty call—

Knock. Knock. Knock.

I reached for my phone on my nightstand, lifted it, checking the screen like it would have answers.

It didn't, unfortunately, because there weren't any missed calls or texts, and while I'd bought a camera doorbell, it was still sitting on my counter—box torn open, contents scattered on the tile, because my apartment had been searched as deeply as my shop had.

Case in point?

I was sleeping on a bare mattress, too tired after everything the night before to search out sheets and pillowcases and remake my bed.

Despite the way I had grown up, it wasn't the first time I'd done that.

When I'd left, I'd left with *nothing*.

Okay, not nothing. I'd taken my car, some clothes, some food from the kitchen.

It had *felt* like nothing with all that I'd had at my fingertips during my childhood.

It had given me something to start off with. I'd lived in my car for six months before I'd saved up enough waitressing to rent a room.

And my father didn't care enough about me to chase me down.

He had his sons. He had his legacy. He could purchase and mold another doll to dress up and play hostess—and she'd probably be a hell of a lot happier about it than I had ever been playing that role.

So...I'd gone, and he'd let me.

And I'd made my own way.

It was only after I turned twenty-five and I'd received notice of my trust that things had gotten easier.

But I didn't want a connection to my father.

So, even though I'd used the money to start Earthly Delights, to buy this building, to make sure I was secure, I hadn't touched it since.

Even if it meant living much smaller than I'd grown up.

Because I'd learned growing up in his huge house, with everything I could ever possibly want and more than most other people had in this world, that my life now was so much bigger. More valuable. More fulfilling.

I had friends, a family I'd built that wasn't blood.

I had work that made me happy.

I had a town where I felt appreciated and not alone and—

And they'd seen me getting hauled off in handcuffs.

Because of Lex Blackwell.

The smolder of my anger ignited, began to burn in my belly, flames licking up through my insides.

That was what propelled me to toss the towel I was using as a blanket back, to shove out of bed, to storm to the front door.

I gripped the handle, yanked it open, and...

Then realized how stupid I'd been.

The man—my father's *criminal defense* attorney—was standing on the porch, suit immaculate, expression beyond irritated, his hand still lifted in preparation to knock again.

"Ms. Lyon," he said with a scowl. "We have much to discuss."

Yeah, no, that wasn't going to happen.

I'd been released. No charges were filed. Lex had said—

I shivered.

Just...*yeah, no.* I was staying far the fuck away from everything to do with my father, letting the FBI do their job, and I was going to live my small, peaceful life.

If my friends didn't disown me, that was.

More flames bursting free.

"We have nothing to discuss," I snapped, whirling away from him and reaching for the door, fingers gripping the edge of the wood as I started to slam it shut.

I got it about six inches before his hand shot up, catching it, preventing me from closing it and then stepping into my space so quickly that I scrambled to back up.

I tripped on something that had been left on the floor, falling backward, nails scrabbling at the wall, like I'd somehow gain purchase on the flat surface.

I didn't.

And the floor was coming up fast.

I braced, already anticipating the pain—

Then the lawyer was shoved out of the way, and warm, rough fingers were wrapping around my wrist...and I...

Stopped falling.

Didn't hit the floor.

My shoulder wrenched, pain shooting down my arm from the force of my descent being halted, but it was only for a moment because then a body had come close, the grip shifting to around my waist, and suddenly I was upright again...and this time pressed to a big, strong chest, held tight by a big, strong man.

Protected. Cared for. Shielded.

My heart pulsed hard.

Because that couldn't be further from the truth.

"Don't fucking touch her," Lex growled.

I exhaled, felt my feet beneath me and carefully started to back away.

The arm around my middle tightened, tucked me further into his side.

"Ms. Lyon and I have much to discuss," the smarmy man said. "And you shouldn't be intervening between an attorney and their client, Agent Blackwell."

Lex's anger radiated through the small space, pulsing waves that made me shiver, even though they weren't directed at me.

But his hold was gentle.

Secure, but gentle.

Just like some part of me always knew he would be.

My heart went again, but I forced myself to push that away, to focus on the shitshow that was taking place in front of me.

"You're not my lawyer," I said, feeling Lex's body go even stiffer next to me. "And I don't have anything to say to you." A beat. "Or to my father."

Fingers tightening on my hip, so tight that I winced, shifted away.

Lex wasn't looking at me—his stare was lasered in on the attorney—but, somehow, he sensed that his grip was too tight because it immediately loosened, those fingers turning gentle, stroking gently, as though he could soothe the small ache there.

"Ms. Lyon—"

"It can't have escaped your notice that I haven't talked to my father in years," I said. "I don't have any interest in ending that streak. Now," I said firmly, trying again to move forward, to reach for the door, but Lex didn't loosen his grip. I glanced up at him, saw that a muscle in his jaw was ticking, turned back, saw that the attorney looked equally as pissed as they engaged in the stare down. "I'm asking you to leave," I said firmly.

Lex's head swiveled, eyes searching mine for one brief, heated moment.

Then he was looked back to the attorney, voice a deep, intense threat. "You heard her."

"Francesca, I'd suggest you reconsider—"

"You *heard* her."

The attorney clamped his mouth shut, shook his head sharply.

Then pivoted and marched down the steps.

Lex slammed it shut, flicked the lock.

Turned to face me, all those waves of intense energy suddenly pointed in my direction.

Shit.

NINE

LEX

I turned away from the door, after making sure it was locked, and stared at Frankie.

She was fucking beautiful in the sunshine—her red hair like fire around her head, her lips pale pink and parted in surprise, her eyes wide pools of emerald green, her lush body clad in a thin pair of shorts, a narrow-strapped tank top that clung to curves.

That demonstrated very clearly she wasn't wearing a bra.

My dick went hard.

Christ.

I was moving toward her before I realized, and by then I'd already backed her against the wall, pressed our bodies together.

Soft.

Small.

Her hands came to my shoulders.

I crouched, intending to pick her up, to wrap those sexy thighs around my waist. I was thinking with my dick, with my animalistic brain.

Pick her up, push those shorts out of the way.

Thrust the fuck home.

Nails bit into my flesh, something that surprised me, something that I didn't expect from the soft and sweet and beautiful woman in front of me. Something that I very much liked.

I wanted those nails biting into my bare skin, scoring red lines down my back, digging into my ass, encouraging me to fuck her harder.

But that wasn't what happened.

Those nails bit in, and then her palms were pushing at my shoulders, shoving me away.

Not gently, but I was deep down into instinct, blood flowing south, and she was small.

Even a firm shove took me a second to process.

But her words didn't.

"Don't you have some other woman to accuse and arrest and fuck with?" Another shove, and this one sunk in. I released her, backed away a step, trying to reconcile her tone with the Frankie I knew. Because her tone...

Cold. Hard. *Not* Frankie.

"Don't—" I muttered.

Her eyes narrowed.

"Don't be like that."

Her nostrils flared, lips pressing flat, then releasing. "*You* made me like that." She reached for the doorknob. "Just—"

I gripped her wrist.

"—let me go," she gritted out.

"Not going to happen, baby." I tugged her closer. "Tell me what's wrong."

She snorted. "Tell you what's wrong." A shake of her head. "Tell *you* what's *wrong.*" She swept out a hand. "Look at this place. Look at my home—" Her voice broke. "Look at what you did. And my s-store is worse."

Guilt—it fucking stung. "Baby—"

"You did that," she whispered. "*You*." A little louder. "I was just living my life and now it's—" She exhaled. "Now, it's ruined."

More guilt, like a thousand tiny cuts.

And I knew—*knew*—she was either the best actor I had *ever* come across or she was telling the truth.

She wasn't involved.

Didn't know about her father.

But—a shadow crossed in front of her face—she hadn't fought believing her father capable of it. Which bore the question...

Why?

Why did she believe me?

Why did she believe *me*—the man who'd deceived her for the last year—over her father?

And what had this woman, who was from the loins of a fucking snake, been through?

"I forgave you," she said, voice dropping again. "I forgave you when you were a jerk to me, and I forgave you when you embarrassed me in front of everyone. But this"—she waved a hand again—"this was way worse. It wasn't embarrassment." Her eyes slid closed. "It was evisceration."

My tongue was glued to the roof of my mouth, regret stealing my words. "Frankie," I rasped.

"You used me." An accusation.

The truth.

"I—"

Her eyes held mine and I found that I couldn't lie to her. "Yes."

A flinch, just a slight one.

And I found that my tongue wasn't working again.

"Right," she murmured, exhaling, and back pressing to the wall, she slipped away from me, moving toward the door, hand lifting toward the handle. "It's always the same, isn't it?"

I frowned.

What was always the same?

People using her?

Men using her?

"Baby," I said, moving toward her again. "What—"

"Last night, you said you didn't know how a person could use another for their own gain." She shook her head. "But you *do* know," she murmured. "You know because you did the same to me."

I stilled.

It wasn't the same. It *wasn't.*

I opened my mouth, closed it, my tongue frozen again, the words not coming, and—

"You gained my trust, made me think you were a friend, made me think you might be mor—" She clamped her teeth together, cutting off the flow of words, giving a sharp shake of her head, making me think that she might have been about to say *more.*

And this was a fucking nightmare.

I exhaled. "Frankie—"

"You used me for a case, to further your career."

"That's not true."

She lifted her brows in question—an arch, icy question I fucking hated, and that I struggled to find a palatable answer to.

Because she was right.

And...she was wrong.

"It's not like you think."

"Then what *is* it like?"

It was the fact that her father had been responsible for nearly fucking up my entire career. It was that he'd placed a woman in my life who'd almost cost me my life, my future, everything I held dear. It was that Francis Lyon didn't give a fuck who he hurt so long as he could make his money, live the way he wanted to live, and continued gobbling up properties and power like a fucking Hungry Hippo.

It was that...

Francis Lyon may have applied that same mercenary style to parenting Frankie.

That she'd grown up beneath the monster's glare.

"What is your mom like?"

She paused, hand on the knob, and glanced back over her shoulder at me. Her brows lifted again but there was less ice in the unspoken question and more curiosity. "Are you telling me that you don't know?"

No, I didn't know.

There wasn't much information about the lovers of Francis Lyon, or about the name on Frankie's birth certificate.

No paper trail.

No sightings.

No known aliases or associates or—

"She died giving birth to me."

That wasn't in the file.

"Yeah," Frankie said. "She gave him three sons and one daughter." A shrug. "Did her job, and bled out. Super convenient for my dad—not having to pay to upkeep her for the rest of her life." Another shrug, the frost back and intense and...I fucking hated it. "Although, it was ultimately *inconvenient* because it took a full decade to mold me, to make sure I was up to the challenge to be the lady of the house."

"Baby—"

"I managed to get there in the end, though." Her smile could have cut glass. "Not ever quite good enough, when he bothered to notice me at all, but a suitable woman to smile and look pretty and service his clients."

I went ramrod stiff. "Service how?"

Was it a growl? Fuck, yeah.

Did it reveal too goddamned much? Fuck, yes, it did.

The ice melted. "Not like that," she said softly.

Relief made my knees shake.

"I had to smile and look pretty and serve them drinks. I had to be well-versed in everything unimportant in order to make *them* feel important." Her hand dropped from the handle. "But I didn't service them like how you're thinking. He made me do a lot of things I hated, but not that. Not—" Her eyes closed.

"What did he make you do?"

The question was torn from me and had her eyes flying open. She studied me for a long moment.

Then she murmured, "He barely knew I existed."

"That doesn't answer my question."

One shoulder lifted, fell. "It doesn't matter."

It fucking did.

It *really* fucking did.

But before I could say that, her hand went back to the knob, and she twisted it, pulled open the door, flooding the room with bright sunshine.

"You should go."

TEN

FRANKIE

My fingers trembled but I made them turn the knob anyway.

He needed to go.

Right then.

I'd already revealed too damned much.

I pulled open the door, the sunlight so bright it was almost a slap in the face. All the turmoil in my belly, in my life, and the sky was cerulean blue. Not a cloud in sight, just a broad expanse of beauty and sunshine glinting off the waves in the distance, my little slice of ocean view on full display.

Normally, I would have paused and breathed, soaked in that moment of peace.

Of home.

Of *mine.*

But...Lex needed to go, and I needed to clean the shop, get it back in order. People were depending on me for products. I needed to do an inventory, order more supplies, get ready for the Girl Scout program I was supposed to be hosting that night.

If they even still came.

If they didn't decide to keep their distance from a woman who'd been hauled off in handcuffs.

"You should go," I said softly, staring out at my chunk of ocean so I didn't get sucked into the man behind me.

Into his eyes, a deep sea blue with flecks of gray that reminded me of the breaking waves.

Into his strength and the easy confidence with which he carried himself.

Into in the fantasy of him.

That this big, strong, capable man might look at me and see...

Someone that wasn't lacking.

Someone who might be his fantasy in return.

"You should—" I began again, right as he moved close...

His hand took mine, peeled it from the knob, his other coming to the wooden panel and slamming it shut.

"Answer my question." A demand. An order.

My lungs seized, but I lifted my chin. "You *need* to go."

He moved closer, until my body was pinned by his against the door. I didn't know if he was harder...or if the wood was, but I found that I couldn't concentrate on any of it, not when he bent, his lips coming to my ear, hot words hitting my senses. "Tell me."

"He didn't do anything," I whispered.

"Bullshit."

"He'd actually have to give a fuck about me in order for that to be a lie," I muttered. "And since he barely knew that I existed, except when I wasn't polite enough or pretty enough or thin enough—"

Fuck.

I clamped my teeth together.

Fingers on my hip, his big body moving me away from the door so he could spin me around. I couldn't avoid his heavy gaze as he arrowed right in on exactly what I didn't want him to, what I'd never meant for him to hear. "*Thin enough?*"

Dammit.

My eyes slid to the side, which was definitely not the right call when it came to dealing with an FBI agent.

"Baby." His hand on my cheek. "*Thin* enough?"

"I had a personal trainer at nine. A chef for as long as I can remember. A stylist and makeup artist, someone who did my hair. A tutor." I didn't go to real school. I couldn't be trusted not to mess up there, couldn't be trusted not to be perfect. "It's the life that people dream of."

A long pause.

"It sounds like a prison," he murmured.

It had been.

One I'd been desperate to escape—once I'd realized that even if I played by the rules, had done everything in my power to be that perfect little girl, perfect teenager, perfect woman for him that nothing would change.

"I was exceptionally privileged," I said softly. "I think you know enough about him to understand that."

"A bird in a golden cage."

I sucked in a breath. "I was fine," I said, needing him to go, needing him to not watch me with that gentle look on his face.

"Were you ever just a kid?"

My lungs froze again.

He cursed, hand sliding from my cheek down to rest on the side of my throat. "Don't bother lying, baby. That breath was answer enough."

I blinked, suddenly wanting to cry again.

"Tell me," he pressed.

My gaze went back to his. I really wished it hadn't because it told me he saw too damned much. I lifted my chin. "You seem to be coming to plenty of your own conclusions."

His mouth quirked, as though me trying to put him off by being snarky amused him.

But only for a moment.

Then he sobered again, that gentle making a reappearance that bored right through me. "Do you still struggle with it?"

My fingers clenched into fists, nails biting into my skin, heart pounding all of a sudden. "I'm fine," I said. "I have a full life. I'm happy."

He reached between us, unfurled one of my fists, then the other. "Are you?" he asked, palm coming back to my cheek. "Are you happy?"

I was...and I wasn't.

His eyes told me he saw that flit through my mind.

"That's what I thought," he murmured. "Because I sure as shit know that your life isn't full."

I flinched. "Why are you so mean?"

Fingers sliding along my jaw, gripping my chin. "I'm not being mean, baby," he murmured. "I've just spent enough time watching you over the last year to know that your life isn't full. You work," he added when I opened my mouth to protest. "You go to your friends' places. You work. You spend time with the Jacksons. You work. You sit on the beach. And—surprise—you come back here and work."

My temper splintered. "I work because I love what I do." I jabbed a finger into his chest. "I love that I get to help people feel better and eat healthier without criticizing that they might have put on a pound or gained an inch. I love that people can have good, high-quality products in their houses or use them for their bodies or on their kids and know that they're safe." I jabbed again. "I love that I can help someone find something to make them sleep better or a healthy snack that they're able to put in their kid's lunch."

His expression had gone soft.

But I couldn't stop the flow of words, couldn't stop

revealing too damned much.

"So, maybe I'm not traveling the world"—not that I ever had, trapped such as I was in my gilded cage—"or handcuffing bad guys or dating my way through Darlington's single population, but I'm doing something worthwhile, I'm doing something that makes me feel good, something I think that's important—*really* freaking important."

More gentle. More soft.

Almost as soft and gentle as the brush of his thumb across my bottom lip, as his words when he said, "You're right."

"And you took that away," I whispered. "You ruined it and no one will look at me the same way. I'll always be that criminal who—"

"Bullshit."

I glared up at him, opened my mouth, but his thumb brushed over my bottom lip again.

"Bullshit, baby," he murmured. "They'll look at you and know that you're the woman who makes special batches of granola for a nursing mom who needs them for a healthy breakfast. The woman who'll teach a bunch of fifth graders how to cook, even though they wreck chaos and destruction in her kitchen. The woman who gets up before the sun because she cares about her work and puts in the time to make her small slice of the world a better place."

I inhaled, eyes burning.

He'd noticed that?

Noticed *all* of that?

"But you thought—"

His cupped my jaw, tilted my head back. "I was wrong. I was an asshole, and...fuck. I was *wrong*." A beat. "I'm so sorry, baby."

My lungs inflated on a huge, shocked inhale. "I—"

But I didn't get a chance to get the rest of my words out.

Because then he was bending close...

And he pressed his mouth to mine.

ELEVEN

LEX

She tasted like warm days on the beach, the spray of the ocean's waves.

She tasted like temptation and sin...

And future.

My future.

I bent and lifted her up, kissing her like I'd wanted to for the last year, from the moment I'd walked into her shop a story below, my cock reacting instantly to the sight of her, the smell of her, the dusting of freckles on her nose and over the tops of her cheeks.

And just like every other time I touched her, my dick was hard and I wanted to strip her naked.

Her thin tank top, those barely their shorts.

That plump ass in my palms. Her soft breasts pressed to my chest.

I wanted to keep kissing her. I *wanted* to fuck her. I wanted to do it fast and deep, slow and steady, driving her insane moment by moment until she surrendered to me.

I wanted to own every inch of her.

She moaned, legs wrapping around my waist, lining our pelvises up.

I got the soft cushion of her pussy against my dick—though, there were way too many fucking layers in between us. I got the vibration of another groan on my tongue. I got her nails biting into my flesh, but for a whole different reason this time.

Normally, she was soft and sweet and gentle.

Funny, but in a quiet way.

Generous in spirit.

But...she kissed like sin.

Her moan vibrating up between us, sliding down my tongue, my stomach, stroking along my cock. Her hips arched and rocked against my pelvis, making me desperate to slid into that tight, wet cunt. Her lips parted, tongue meeting mine, hands sliding up and down my body—one going to my ass, pulling her even more tightly against me, the other slipping beneath the hem of my T-shirt, nails raking across my flesh.

Soft and sweet and gentle...but underneath a wildcat.

A fucking tigress.

I moved, turning us away from the door, doing my best to not step on shit as I brought us to the bed, as I laid her down on it—

As I paused.

Pulled back.

Took in what she was lying on.

"Why don't you have any blankets on your bed, baby?"

It was just a bare mattress, one pillow without a case, a terrycloth towel bunched to the side.

The desire cleared from her eyes in a second, head swiveling, gaze taking in her apartment. "They took them off," she whispered.

Guilt slicing through me. *Again.*

"And they're dirty." Another whisper. "Boot prints—"

Fuck.

"Shit, baby, I'm sorry."

Her gaze turned back and she studied my face for long, long seconds. Then her palm pressed flat to my cheek. "You really mean that, don't you?"

The utter surprise in her words was another fucking slice, but I just peeled her hand from my face, pressed a kiss to the center of it. Part of me demanded that I pull back, that I tell her, no, I didn't mean that.

Fear demanded that I state I was still suspicious, that I knew she was like her father, *knew* she was like—

Her.

Hailey.

But I wasn't a fucking idiot, even though I'd spent a decent chunk of time stepping into that role lately.

Frankie wasn't Hailey.

As much as that would make things easier.

"I do mean that," I told her.

Her utter shock at my agreement confirmed it. I inhaled, searching for words—

She arched up and sealed her mouth over mine, tongue sliding between my lips, kissing me hot and deep and wet and...*dirty.*

Beautifully fucking dirty.

I groaned and rolled us, taking the bare mattress, taking my weight, making sure she didn't get crushed, allowing myself better access to her curves...

And that was the moment she went *wild.*

Hands yanking me up to sitting, ripping my sweatshirt off, my tee off, tossing them to the side as her mouth hit my chest, nails raked over my skin, lips latched onto my nipple. I groaned, one hand diving into her hair, keeping her against me as I slid my hand beneath her tank, cupped her breast, rolling her nipple back and forth between thumb and forefinger.

"Fuck," she gasped, hips grinding against me, head arching back.

Yes. That.

I wanted it.

But this was the wrong time, the wrong moment—and I didn't have a condom.

Even as I had that thought, her hands went to the waistband of my sweats, shoved them and my underwear down.

My cock sprang free.

"Baby—"

Then her mouth latched *there* and I seriously fucking hated the fact that I didn't have a condom. Because her mouth was hot and slick, and she was sucking me so hard and deep, and I was desperate to be in that pussy of hers.

"Frankie—" She did something with her tongue and I groaned, head falling back to the mattress.

Tempted, so fucking tempted.

I groaned again...

Then pulled her off, tugged her up, fingers diving into her shorts, seeking out her clit, the slick folds, showing her as much mercy as she'd shown me...which was to say *none.*

"Oh, God," she moaned, hips bucking. "Oh, my *God.*"

"That's it, tigress," I coaxed. "Fucking ride my fingers, baby. Come on my hand."

She jerked, pussy clenching around me—

But then she was off my fingers.

"Baby—"

She reached up, past my head. A drawer opened, contents rattled, and a second later, I saw that she'd pulled out a condom.

There was a God.

I tore it open, rolled it along the length of my cock.

She shoved her shorts down.

"On me, baby," I ordered as she straddled my hips. "Get me inside you."

Then she was doing as I commanded, my head notching at her entrance, sliding down, sheathing me in tight, slick heat.

"Oh God," she groaned, head flopping back, hips moving, pelvis grinding against mine.

My thumb went to her clit, pressing and circling, feeling her convulse, watching her tits bounce as she fucked me hard and fast and deep.

Then that hot, slick cunt was tightening around me, pulsing as she came apart, sending any bit of control I had out of my head. It snapped, and I flipped us again, pounding into her, fast and furious and without quarter, taking what I'd wanted for so damned long.

Needing to claim her.

Needing to take.

Needing to—

Come.

I exploded, probably holding her too tight, probably going too fast, but when I came out of that haze of pleasure, she was clinging to me just as fiercely.

"You okay?" I whispered when I could speak again.

"I don't know what came over me," she whispered, and I leaned up, saw that her cheeks were pink.

"I don't know either," I said, smoothing my hand along her side, "but I'm damned glad it did."

She froze.

I chuckled.

"It's never—" Cheeks going even more pink. "I never been like that with a man—" She clamped her lips together, but fuck if that didn't make me feel like I'd just killed a grizzly with my bare hands, or climbed Everest, or defeated Thanos and a spate of aliens.

She'd been like that...

Only with me.

I liked it—probably too fucking much. "Frankie—"

She yawned and my heart convulsed.

"Did you get any sleep last night?"

"I'm fine." She started to shove her hair out of her face. "I should"—another yawn—"get up. I have a lot"—one more—"to do and everything's still a mess."

She needed to sleep, but I didn't think she'd take me ordering her to stay in bed well.

Not when we'd just found a bit of peace.

And pleasure.

And—

She yawned again, and I tightened my arms, tugged her back against me, running my hand along her side, lightly and repeatedly, until her body relaxed, until she wasn't yawning but her eyes were sliding closed and she'd slumped heavily against me.

Lips parting, breaths coming in soft puffs.

Fucking cute.

Fucking *beautiful*.

My heart squeezed hard, panic and regret, guilt and need all twisted together.

I still didn't move though.

Just held her until I was certain that she slept.

Then I slipped from the bed and I took care of the condom, pulled my sweats back up, and maybe I should have left, should have gone home, gotten on with my life, pretended that this didn't happen.

But seeing Frankie sprawled out on the mattress, beautiful body on display and I couldn't go anywhere but back into that bed, sliding in behind her, tugging her close.

Minutes, hours later, my phone buzzed in my back pocket, and I still didn't want to pull back, didn't want to release her from my hold.

I did anyway.

Because of those twisted emotions.

Because I couldn't put my life on hold for a woman—not ever again.

Carefully slipping my arms free so I didn't wake her, I pushed off the bed and stood there, staring down at her, at the steady breathing, the lashes forming half-moons on the tops of her cheeks.

Naked.

Curvy.

Beautiful.

Mine.

I ground my teeth together, seeing goose bumps appear on her skin and I hated that the fucking mattress was still bare, hated that the only thing I had to cover her up with was that damned towel. I grabbed my sweatshirt from where she'd tossed it on the ground, gently smoothed it over her.

Then I covered her with the fucking towel.

TWELVE

FRANKIE

I don't know what woke me, long hours later.

Maybe it was the fact that the sun was high in the sky, shining really brightly through the windows.

Maybe it was that I was finally hungry, my stomach grumbling loudly enough to wake the dead.

Maybe it was that I was cold, and I awoke to an empty bed.

Sighing, I sat up, rubbing my eyes.

Seeing that Lex was gone.

My stomach twisted, and maybe I would have thought it was all a stupid, ridiculous fantasy...if not for the fact that I was naked in my bed and my apartment was a mess and—

His sweatshirt was bunched around my middle.

With the towel I'd used as a blanket last night.

My hand shook as I lifted it, reaching for the cotton, feeling the soft material beneath my fingertips, dragging it up to my nose and inhaling.

Spice. Male. *Lex.*

I'd smelled it on his skin, smelled it as his body wrapped around mine, smelled it as I fell asleep in his arms.

Something that was a dream...

And a nightmare.

Because my bed was bare, my apartment was torn apart, my shop was a mess...

And my life was still in shambles.

I pulled the sweatshirt over my head, that spice encompassing me, holding me, shielding me...

Like he'd done at the apartment door, like he'd done as I slept, like he'd done—

My fingers landed on a piece of paper, its crinkle drawing my eyes down.

Had to go into work. I'll see you later.

Hope you slept well, baby.

-L

Baby.

From cold eyes to endearments.

I was spinning.

It was the fantasy I'd always wanted.

And yet...I wanted more.

I wanted everything.

Had been obsessed since first glance, was wrecked that it had all been fake, that he seemed to hate me...

Except, he didn't really hate me, did he?

Only, what if it were all bullshit, just another ploy to take down my father?

I mean, I didn't care. My father had made the bed he was lying in. He could deal with the consequences.

It was just...my heart that I was scared for.

And I'd all but jumped Lex, had opened my body to him and for what? An apology, intervening with a smarmy lawyer, a really hot kiss?

He'd betrayed me and lied and my store and apartment were—

I groaned.

"Stupid, Frankie," I muttered, getting out of bed, moving to my tiny closet and pulling on some clothes.

That was the bottom line.

I was stupid for wanting him while knowing the truth.

And stupid for wanting more.

And...I still had my store to clean up.

The apartment could wait.

I needed to get back to work.

That was it.

That was the mission I needed. The focus.

Nodding to myself, I turned on the shower, tugged off the sweatshirt, and I made a vow to put Lex out of my mind.

The sex had been fantastic.

Everything leading up to it had been complete and total bullshit.

So, like I'd done my entire life, I clung onto the grain of good, the slice of positive, and I got on with my life.

But I still felt those roughened fingertips on my skin, the stretch and slight burn between my legs as I washed.

And I still hung that hoodie up in my closet, the spicy scent of him lingering in the air.

And I still couldn't let go of the fantasy.

———

It wasn't until I went to start a load of laundry that I realized he'd thrown my sheets and blankets into the washer.

———

It wasn't until I saw the empty box on the counter that I realized he'd installed my camera doorbell.

———

It wasn't until I turned back around and really surveyed the space that I realized he'd cleaned up my apartment while I slept.

———

And it wasn't until I went downstairs, my heart pounding in anticipation at what I knew instinctually that I would find.

My shop was clean.

Sparkling, completely *clean*.

And my basket of hemp bows was sitting—full—on the counter.

———

Despite my shop being clean, there was still a lot of work to get it functioning again.

Mostly restocking, but I also had to make all new batches of brownies and granola and breakfast cookies—hoping as I did it that I'd actually have people come in to buy them.

Because...I had a group chain of text messages I'd ignored—not able to bring myself to read them.

I had phone calls I'd let go to voicemail. Repeatedly.

And I wanted to tell myself that my friends, the family I'd made would eventually run out of patience for my avoidance, would show up, pound down my door. I wanted to tell myself that they were just giving me a moment to catch my breath...

But what if my friends *didn't* show up?

What if—

The knocking at the back door of my shop was almost comical, sounding loudly and making me jump as it burst through my senses. I nearly upended my bowl of granola, and I took a breath before I carefully straightened it, slid it away from the danger zone that was the edge of my large stainless steel prep table.

I moved to the sink, washed my hands, glancing at the phone I kept there (and well away from the food I prepped—hello, food safety rules), seeing the flurry of messages and calls on the screen.

My stomach went fluttery.

Because, of course, they'd shown up.

And it had taken them all of a day to get tired of me keeping them at a distance.

Now they were blowing up my phone—

Knock. Knock. Knock.

And knocking on my door.

I dried my hands on a paper towel and moved out of the kitchen, down the hall, and to the back door.

Which I barely got open before my friends were barreling inside, Misty first, grabbing me and pulling me into a tight hug, like the sweet, soft, beautiful woman she was, asking, "Are you okay?"

Maggie, my bright, bold, beautiful friend, tugged me from Misty's hold. "How dare you not call us!" She wrapped me tight in her arms. "Also, oh my God, are you okay?"

Raven reached past her, touched my cheek. "Lex is dead to me." A beat. "Again."

I slipped from Maggie's hug, gave Raven a squeeze. "I'm okay. Really," I added when they both just stared at me. "Come back to the kitchen," I told them. "I'll explain everything."

Kim slipped through the door, a broom in one hand. "You don't need to feed us. I've got food in the car and Chance"—her brother-in-law and a local PI—"said this place was a mess."

It had been.

"It's good," I started, but the troops had been mobilized and my friends were parading out the door, returning with brooms and trash bags and buckets of cleaner.

And food.

I smelled the yummy undertones of the diner in the air.

They marched right by me, down the hall, and I felt their surprise as they halted, as they took in the same thing I'd taken in only a couple of hours before.

Which was when there was a shadow in the doorway, and I bit back a gasp, because just as quickly as it appeared, the shadow turned into Rob, Misty's brother. He had a tool belt over one shoulder, a drill in one hand.

"Hey, sweetheart," he murmured. "You good?"

I'd been okay.

Now, I was *good*.

There were so many things wrong with my life—discovering the truth about my father, my conflicted feelings about Lex, the way everything had gone down, the sex that had been the best I'd ever—*ever*—had.

All that mattered right now was that my friends were here. My store was clean.

My door was about to get fixed.

"I'm good," I said softly.

He lifted a brow.

"Or I'm getting there," I admitted.

"Hmm."

I curled my toes into my shoes, bracing for an inquisition, knowing that there was no way I'd avoid one with my friends, but not wanting to face another from a man who was nice and kind, but who also had a spine of steel—or else, he wouldn't have snagged the most famous actress in the world as his wife.

He sighed softly, touched my shoulder. "Would it get you a little closer to that *good*, if I fixed your door?"

Nibbling at my bottom lip, I nodded.

A kiss on my cheek before he moved by me. "Then that's what I'll do."

He'd no sooner cleared the gaggle at the mouth of the hall before my friends turned back to me. Maggie was first, marching toward me, taking my wrist, and dragging me into the stock room. "Okay," she ordered once she'd flicked on the light, sending us all blinking against the sudden blindness. "You were a stubborn bitch and cleaned up while ignoring our offers of help, but a lot of your shelves are empty and those walls need patching. Rob!" she shouted. "We need wall help when you're done with the door!"

"I—"

"On it!" he shouted back before I could get any further along in my refusal.

Mags fixed me with a glare. "So now that's taken care of, you're going to put us to work restocking."

"I—"

She scowled. "No arguments, missy."

My friends nodded in agreement.

And...for the first time since Lex had busted through my door, I knew that I really *was* good.

That I really *would* be okay.

"I'll take you up on my restocking," I said.

"Good—"

I took the broom from Kim.

"But let's eat first," I said, taking her hand. "Because I have so much to tell you."

Thirteen

Lex

I was in my office, staring at my computer, my cock at half-mast—like it had been all fucking day, ever since I'd left Frankie sleeping in her bed.

I'd called in a favor in the form of Attie—she'd met me at Frankie's shop, had helped me clean up, even though she was well within her rights to tell me to fuck off. But when I'd told her I'd be in later, asked her to cover for me at the meeting I was supposed to be attending, she'd jumped at the opportunity.

To initiate me.

To be the number one fan of the Team Frankie fan club.

To see what her store looked like from the inside.

She'd been back at the department, watching Francis's interrogation, doing additional research while the rest of our team had gone through Frankie's shop and apartment, so she'd missed her opportunity. She'd cataloged what we'd brought in, sent appropriate stuff off to the tech team to process further, and because she was a kickass interrogator, she'd sent questions to be asked to the interrogation team, had advised when to let Frankie's father stew, when to push.

The only reason she wasn't in the room at all was because Francis was a known misogynist.

We'd save that particular button to push for another time.

Because we *had* time.

The charges had been filed, bail had been denied, and now it was time to run with all the pieces we'd been slowly sliding into place. We'd been taken by surprise and needing to act quickly with Francis's unannounced appearance in Frankie's shop, but the prep work was there.

We'd worked our asses off.

Now Francis Lyon was going to pay.

But all of that was running in the background of my mind.

Mostly because Attie had taken one look at me and gotten gleeful. "I fucking knew it," she'd crowed. "Knew you would see it my way."

Frankie.

Christ, I *was* seeing it Attie's way.

I couldn't even blame it on my dick, pretend I was a young pup to be led around by it like I had been with Hailey.

I'd known Frankie for a year.

I tried to keep walls up, tried to keep my distance.

I should have known it was hopeless the first time she smiled up at me.

Exhaling, I locked the case file, pushed out of my chair, grabbed my wallet and keys, shoved my phone in my pocket, and I walked out the door knowing that it was probably really fucking stupid to believe her, really stupid to be falling for her—

But knowing I wasn't going to stop.

I was walking out of my office, to the elevator, to my car, knowing that I wasn't going back to my apartment.

I was going to Earthly Delights.

To tease out the mystery of Frankie Lyon.

Because the alternative was to end up like I had before.

And no matter how innocent and sweet and beautiful Frankie was, I wasn't going to allow her to destroy my life.

———

I pulled into the parking lot and saw that fucking rock was propping the back door open.

She'd been all but accosted by her father's attorney, Shane Henderson—the sleazy fuck—and now she was leaving the back door to her shop open?

I don't know how I intended to handle the situation before seeing that rock—those intentions flitted away like so much smoke before I'd cleared my car door. I slammed the metal panel shut, blipped the locks, strode for that open door.

The hallway light was on, but it didn't do shit, especially with the door to the interior staircase leading up to her apartment wide open, the hall beyond dark.

My anger ramped. My vision went hazy.

Anyone could walk in.

Anyone.

And her fucking father was Francis Lyon, so seriously, any *fucking* person could come in, could surprise her, could *hurt* her, and she wouldn't even—

I kicked the fucking rock out of the way, letting the door slam shut.

When it did, I realized I'd been hearing voices down the hall, voices that cut off with that slam.

I was too pissed to care.

It didn't matter that she wasn't alone.

In fact, it was worse. That meant that even more of them were being fucking stupid by not closing the fucking door, by not making sure it was locked.

Jesus Christ.

I strode into the kitchen, took in the pack of women.

Jesus *fucking* Christ.

I lifted my cell, jabbed at the screen, not having missed when I drove by that the lights had been on in Chance and Carter's office. It rang once.

"Lex," Carter snapped, "you've been avoiding my calls and we need to talk, asshole."

I *had* been avoiding Carter's calls.

I *was* an asshole.

But both of those were the least of my worries right at that moment.

"You and your brothers' women are here with *my* woman, and they're all cackling around the table in Frankie's kitchen with the fucking back door propped open where anyone might come in and..." I let that trail off because Carter knew enough to fill in the blanks, because the women in front of me were staring wide-eyed and slack jawed.

Because my woman—Jesus *fucking* Christ—was watching me with her kissable mouth parted in surprise, those deep green eyes locked onto me.

"Fuck," Carter muttered. "I'll be there in a minute."

Yeah, he would.

I pulled the phone away from my ear, jabbed at the screen, shoved it in my pocket.

And then I lifted my brows at the gathering of women.

Raven moved first, eyes narrowing in my direction, but I saw that Frankie had told her enough that I didn't have *too* big of a hole to dig out of with her. She pushed her stool back, stood, and started gathering up her stuff, Misty, Kim, and Maggie following suit.

"We'll let you two talk," Raven murmured, sliding past me.

Frankie started to get up.

I narrowed my eyes.

Her ass hit the seat again.

Then, because I was an asshole, but I was one who gave a shit about these women being safe, I moved, got in front of them, and was there before the knock sounded on the door. I cracked it, glared out into the opening at Carter, and allowed the women to transfer into his safekeeping.

"We need to talk," he snapped.

"Tomorrow," I snapped back.

His eyes flashed.

I'm sure mine flashed right back.

Then he cursed under his breath, shook his head, and let the door slam shut.

I muttered my own curse, walked back down the hall, and into the kitchen.

And that was when I lost it.

Fourteen

"...And I didn't know," I whispered, my fingers tracing the narrow indent that ran along the edge of the steel prep table. I chanced a look up at them, braced for the derision in their gazes.

But that's not what I found.

Raven's eyes sparked with fury—but then again, she knew what it was like to have an evil person be a parent.

Misty's glimmered with tears—because she had a heart of gold and couldn't imagine what it was like, not with a good man like Rob as her only parental figure.

Kim's was a combination of both—because she'd been through the shit, but she also had a big, beautiful heart.

And Maggie...well, Maggie was prepared to take her rage to my father's mansion, pitchforks and torches in hand.

Even Soph had FaceTimed in and was looking equally furious.

And...God, I loved my friends.

"We know," Misty said, reaching over the table and taking my hand. "Honey, we *know.*"

"The only question is"—Maggie placed her hand over ours—"why you didn't think it was safe to tell us all that before?"

I exhaled. "I—" My eyes stung and I shook my head.

Misty's fingers squeezed mine. "It's okay."

"No," I whispered. "It's not. I glossed over my family because... they might be related to me, but they're not my family. Because I love you guys, and you're way more of one to me than they ever were."

"Honey—"

Her voice broke.

Hell, even Maggie looked close to tears.

This was why I didn't want to add my black clouds to the mix. They were all living in the bright. They were all living their happy endings.

I didn't need my drama dragging everything down.

"Okay," I said lightly. "So, those are the skeletons in my closet, and that's why I was handcuffed and dragged out to an unmarked sedan."

"I mean," Raven said, jumping on my moment of levity. "Just saying, I wouldn't mind exploring the concept of handcuffs with one Lex Blackwell."

Sophie cackled through the phone.

Kim smacked Raven.

Misty just sighed and shook her head.

"I love you guys," I whispered.

Now Misty sniffed, and she wasn't the only one. We were all close to tears, which was probably why Maggie said, "Tell me more about Lex and the handcuffs."

My cheeks went pink.

Because that had me thinking about handcuffs and a big, strong body, a thick cock thrusting home, my hands bound above my head, not able to touch.

Solely at the mercy of Lex Fucking Blackwell.

It would be...glorious.

"Oh my God," Soph said, her voice echoing through the speakers of Misty's phone. "You've been bad, Frankie girl, and it's nothing to do with handcuffs."

My cheeks went even hotter.

Maggie whooped. "But it's definitely to do with Lex—"

The exterior door slammed and I jumped, all of our gazes whipping toward the hall, as though we could see through walls and shadows and—

"Do you think that's the wind or your—" Kim lifted her hands, balancing them like scales.

I bit my bottom lip. "Wind, right?" I murmured. "It's got—"

The shadows moved.

I gasped.

Lex materialized—like a monster...or a god.

He was definitely god-like with his powerful stride, with the way he took up space. It was intense, his mere presence as he walked into the kitchen, one arm lifted, hand holding his cell, pressing it to his ear. "You and your brothers' women are here with *my* woman, and they're all cackling around the table in Frankie's kitchen," he snapped. "*With* the fucking back door propped open where anyone might come in and..."

Shit.

We'd left the door open?

We'd spent the last few hours restocking while Rob had fixed my door and my walls, and that meant we'd all made several trips to the dumpster—both to dispose of cardboard and trash and to throw out an entire box of food that had been contaminated, their seals not properly holding.

I hated to throw it out.

But I couldn't sell it.

And the company wouldn't take it back—something I knew, unfortunately, from experience.

So, it was destined for the trash.

And...apparently, we'd left the door open after that final trip, Rob having escaped the womanly gathering (probably with a significant amount of relief) much earlier.

My shop was back together.

My life was still up in the air.

And Lex was *pissed*.

He pulled the phone away from his ear, jabbed at the screen —conversation apparently over—and shoved it in my pocket.

Then he lifted his brows...and hell if I didn't feel that like it was a stroke between my legs.

My thighs trembled.

My pussy went wet.

My words stoppered up in the back of my throat.

Raven recovered first—ER doc instincts for the win. Although, those instincts and her actions weren't too much in my favor. Mostly because she pushed her stool back, stood, and started gathering up her stuff, Misty, Kim, and Maggie following suit.

"We'll let you two talk," Raven said in a low tone, moving toward to hall.

Leaving me.

Abandoning me to the god-like fury and strength of one Lex Blackwell.

I started to get up.

Lex narrowed his eyes.

My thighs trembled again, and my ass hit the seat again, fingers lifting to the edge of the table, clinging to the metal, the cold steadying me.

But not clearing my head.

Because he followed my friends out, disappearing into the hall, and I heard sharp voices echo down it.

Then the door slammed again and I realized I'd been sitting there for too long.

I should have gotten up.

I should have left.

I should—

Lex came back in, his fury hitting me first.

"What the fuck were you thinking?" he roared, fist pounding on the table, the metal *thwack* echoing through the air.

Maybe that should have made me cower, to shrink back.

But—for some reason, with this man, the sight of his fury didn't diminish me. It ignited me. I pushed back from the table, shot up to my feet. "Don't you yell at me," I snapped. "I'm not a child to be disciplined."

A muscle ticked in his jaw. "You left that fucking door wide open." His nostrils flared on an inhale. "After what happened this morning, after what you found out about your father, you left that fucking door open when you know, *know* he and his associates could be dangerous to you."

"I—"

He made a point.

Which I hated.

But he did.

"Okay," I said. "You're right. I need to be more careful."

"By keeping your fucking doors shut and locked, by not being alone in this store when it's open"—I started to protest, but he wasn't done, striding toward me, walking me back so I was pressed between his body and the stainless-steel door of the fridge—"by promising me that you won't take any more fucking moonlit walks on the beach."

My teeth clacked together.

That anger sat heavy in my belly.

"And what," I muttered, lifting my hands and shoving at his

chest—which did fuck-all to move his big body. "You're offering to escort me when I need to clear my head?"

His hand lifted, so fast that I should have probably flinched.

But somehow, I didn't.

I knew.

Knew he wouldn't hurt me.

And how messed up did that make me?

But he didn't strike me or slap me or *hurt* me, just settled his palm on the side of my throat, thumb extending up to brush along my jaw. "Yeah, baby," he murmured. "That's *exactly* what I'm offering."

And then...

He kissed me.

FIFTEEN

LEX

"Yeah," I muttered to Attie, cell pressed to my ear, trying to ignore the glee in her tone that I'd finally admitted to the inevitable. "I think it's time to take me off the case."

This being because I'd kissed Frankie down in that kitchen of hers, barely resisting the urge to lift her onto the stainless-steel table and fuck her senseless.

I'd only resisted because the table was cold and hard...

And Frankie and I needed to have a conversation.

She needed to know shit, she needed to make the choice, and she needed information so she could stop leaving doors open and walking at midnight on the beach and keep herself fucking *safe*.

"I'll take care of it," Attie said. Then she paused, and I heard her glee transform into genuine curiosity...and concern.

I inhaled, braced.

"How deep?" she asked quietly.

I glanced over at the woman I'd become fucking obsessed with.

Frankie was sitting on her couch—a couch I'd watched her sit on through my binoculars, watched her read late into the night, watched her fall asleep in front of the TV, watched her sit with her gaggle of friends cackling as they downed bottles of wine.

She looked thoroughly fucked.

I hadn't gotten there yet.

But...we'd kissed, and we'd done it long enough that she had sex hair and swollen lips and whisker burn on her throat.

And her shirt was on backward.

No matter, I'd fix that in a bit.

"Deep," I told Ats quietly. "Too fucking deep."

A sigh that rattled through the speakers. "I want to say be careful," she murmured. "But I think that's exactly what you need." A beat, amusement creeping into her tone. "Getting deep."

The tension—the worry, the fucking panic I was trying to pretend wasn't there—broke. "Seriously?" I muttered.

"I'm a child," she said matter-of-factly, "but that doesn't mean you don't appreciate my sense of humor."

Normally, I appreciated it a whole fucking lot.

Right then, when I'd just traversed a narrow plank strung across a fucking gorge below, teetering as I tiptoed my way across...

I wasn't feeling it.

Especially when I'd just glanced up and saw that there was an even longer plank, an even deeper gorge to cross.

"Start making the arrangements," I said instead of agreeing with her. "I'll talk to the boss tomorrow."

She wouldn't like it, my supervisor.

But she'd get it.

And would appreciate me tabling the bullshit, leveling with her, and making sure I didn't fuck up the case we'd all worked so fucking hard on.

"Right." Another beat and I could practically hear Attie's laughter, even before it began.

"Christ," I muttered, lifting the phone from my ear, intending to end the call before—

"Enjoy *getting deep.*"

Yup. I fucking knew it.

"Jesus, Attie," I muttered.

"Don't—"

I hung up, relieved that I cut off her protest about using that nickname and feeling no little amount of pleasure at getting at least one small thing up on her.

The woman was devious.

And fucking incredible—smart, quick, talented, hell of a shot.

And...*devious.*

Sighing, I pocketed my cell, turned back to Frankie, still sitting wide-eyed on the couch. "You know how many times I watched you sit on that couch, baby?"

Her eyes went wider. "Wh-what?"

"I used to stand in the shadows of my bedroom"—I nodded toward the windows, toward where I could see the outline of my apartment, the interior dark and filled with those shadows I spoke of—"I used to watch you, wait for you to *prove* that you were just like your father."

She inhaled sharply.

"I watched you read so many books, baby."

Now she exhaled, and I moved toward her, settled on the couch next to her, then promptly decided that I fucking hated the distance between us and pulled her into my lap. She could have fought—considering how I'd treated her and how I'd barked at her and what I'd just admitted to doing—could have pulled back and refused to allow me to touch her.

But she was Frankie.

She was soft and sweet and yeah there was fire and steel, but ultimately, her insides were gentle, caring, *Frankie.*

So not her father.

I'd been delusional even pretending to think she was.

"I watched you with the girls while you all ate up that shitty reality TV you love. I watched you sleep. And," I murmured. "I watched you cook a special batch of granola for Mrs. Peterson after you'd closed the shop for the day, followed when you delivered it to her house."

Her mouth opened and she exhaled.

It was shaky.

"I watched you for months and I waited for you to show your true self, and I did that because I've been fucked over by a woman before. A woman who seemed soft and sweet and too fucking good to be true…"

Her expression gentled.

"And it turned out that your father had planted her in my life."

She gasped.

"We had an ongoing investigation," I said. "Her job was to be a honeypot, to make me fall for her, and to fuck up our work." Anger boiled in my belly. "It worked too. That chain of investigation was interrupted, corrupted, and I nearly lost my job."

Another gasp, quieter this time, paired with her eyes going glassy.

"So, when I learned that Francesca Lyon had befriended *my* family, my best friends, I arranged to come back, to transfer to a different office. My squad came with me—they're committed as I am—and we began digging deep." I wiped at her lashes, at the tear clinging there.

"I'm sorry," she whispered.

"I know." I cupped her jaw. "And it's not your fault, baby. I know you didn't know about your father. Or about Hailey."

"I—" She blinked rapidly. "I can talk to his attorney, see if I can find anything out to help you guys, something to help the investigation—"

"*No.*"

She flinched at my tone and I had to be careful, really fucking careful to keep my hold gentle. "No, baby. Shane Henderson—your father's attorney—is a fucking shark. He saw you with me. He couldn't miss me intervening. He won't give us anything good, and he might plant something that could hurt the case." I shook my head, slid my hand down until it settled on the side of her neck. I squeezed lightly, made sure she was a hundred percent focused on me. "More than that, baby, he works for your father, and your father is a dangerous man. He runs drugs. He runs people. And when associates inform on him, they disappear."

She shivered.

But I pushed on, needing her to understand exactly how dangerous this was. "No bodies found. No trace remaining. They just...disappear."

Another shiver. "I didn't know." She licked her lips, swallowed hard. "I mean, I knew he wasn't good. I knew he didn't love me for me, but I never would have thought—"

Her voice broke.

"I know, baby." I squeezed lightly again. "You're a good person. *How* could you believe that he would do something like this?"

She shook her head. "I don't know. But I should have."

I touched her cheek. "Which brings this conversation back to us."

She gulped. Audibly.

Then squeaked, "*Us?*"

Sixteen

FRANKIE

My heart was pounding.

Because...*us?*

His hand tightened on my throat, not scaring me, not hurting me, not intimidating.

But it did have me thinking about all sorts of things that didn't fit into this conversation—how that hand could tighten as he was poised over my naked body, how he could hold me in place as he did what he wanted to me, how that hand might slide down, tightening over other body parts, spreading my thighs, slipping those thick, blunt fingers inside my—

"What just went through your mind?"

I blinked, cheeks going hot.

They were probably bright red, which was a freaking sight to see when it came to being a redhead.

"Baby," he murmured.

I shivered again, that voice rasping down my middle, settling right between my legs, stroking—

His hand slid down—over my shoulder, along my arm, dropping onto the indent of my hip.

A tug, and I was even closer.

I opened my mouth, almost blurted out the thoughts, the fantasies. But I had the feeling that would be like opening Pandora's box, sending a cascade of thoughts out through my mouth, until I was exposed and vulnerable and he knew exactly how much I liked him.

Although, I suspected he already knew that.

It wasn't like I'd played it cool. I'd spent my fair share of the last year mooning over him, staring at him, and—

"You don't like me," I blurted, grasping at straws so I didn't reveal everything I'd held inside my heart for so long.

He chuckled. "*That's* what you've got from this conversation?"

I—

Well...um...

My throat dried up. "I—"

A brush of his mouth over my forehead. "My problem has always been that I liked you *too* much."

Heat on my cheeks, in my belly, between my legs. "I—"

"You're not like her," he said quietly, hips flexing, drawing me closer. "I was too much of an idiot to see it before, too fucking stubborn to recognize that Carter and Chance and the rest of the Jacksons wouldn't have allowed a snake into their family."

That stung.

His hand came back to my cheek. "It wasn't you," he murmured. "I was too close to it, baby. I didn't trust them, and I didn't trust myself."

"Lex—"

"Because when I did before, it went really fucking wrong. And, frankly, because my team and I have worked really hard to take your dad down."

Because he was a criminal.

Because he wasn't just a controlling asshole who had fucked-up views of women.

He traded in people and sold drugs and profited off the lives of others.

I...didn't know how to reconcile that with my upbringing, but, also, as I sat in that, in what Agent Phillips had told me and what Lex had confided in me, I began remembering things.

Meetings and skeevy men.

Being swept away to my bedroom.

Raised voices.

And once...what must have been a gunshot.

My nanny had said a picture had fallen off the wall, but I'd never seen one out of place, never spotted one with broken glass or a frame that was dented.

Everything was always...perfect.

Like I'd never been.

"I see you," Lex murmured, lifting his other arm, cupping my jaw. "I see you and I promise I won't forget that."

I inhaled, long and deep and fast, holding the air in my lungs until my vision began to darken at the edges.

Then I released it, and said softly, "Thank you."

A nod, his hold tightening just the slightest bit. "And I care about you."

Another of those long, fast, deep inhales. "I like you too, Lex," I admitted, feeling like I was jumping out of a plane without a parachute, just diving into the clear blue cerulean sky. I lifted my chin, forced myself to meet his eyes. "But you knew that already."

A hint of mischief in deep blue eyes. A mouth twitching beneath a thick, dark beard. "Yeah, baby, I did. Now," he said before I could die of embarrassment, hand sliding down, lightly gripping the side of my neck again, sending that pulse of heat through my middle, those barrage of fantasies through my mind. "Where does your mind go when I do this?"

"I—"

Wicked joining mischief and making me melt.

"I've had sex before," I blurted.

And...yup. Commence dying of embarrassment.

Especially when he lifted a brow. "That thought *did* cross my mind, baby." He leaned in, brushed his lips over mine, voice going husky. "Right about the time I was balls deep inside that tight pussy of yours."

I gasped. "*Lex.*

His fingers tightened again, the other hand sliding down and *in*, skimming over my breasts, my middle, stopping just above the waistband of my pants. "I think you like it when I talk about that pretty pink pussy, baby."

I gasped again.

But also...I did like it.

Really liked it.

"And I want to talk about it." His fingers slipped beneath the waistband of my pants, rough skin brushing over my flesh, sending tremors through my body, moisture between my legs. "I want to be back in there feeling that slick, hot cunt of yours gripping my cock tight again."

Oh, God.

I was going to pass out.

"But, baby, we've got more to talk about." His hand at my throat flexed. "Breathe, baby."

I let out a shuddering breath.

"Good," he murmured, thumbing stroking up and down over my rapidly increasing pulse. "Now," he ordered softly. "Don't lose that look in your eyes, don't lose that heat, baby, because we're going to get back to it."

My pulse increased further, increased until I was almost dizzy with need. "O-okay," I whispered.

"I need to talk to you seriously about Henderson and your father," he said. "They're dangerous and you truly need to be careful, need to make sure you lock your doors and not take extra risks. Even from jail, your father has a long reach, okay?"

I swallowed against my tight throat. "Okay."

"Good, baby." He brushed his mouth over mine again. "Attie is taking lead on the case and I'm stepping back because I can't be"—he squeezed lightly again—"I can't be like this with you and not jeopardize what my squad has worked for."

"I—" I pressed my lips together. "Do you not want to be with me?" I asked softly, then hurried to add because I realized what that sounded like. "I don't mean it as a threat or that I'm insecure—"

Though God knew, my head was spinning when it came to Lex and his interest and the sex and the fact that he'd liked me for a long time, but had been ignoring it because—

He thought I was like my father.

And suddenly, it was critically important that I make sure he knew...

I wasn't.

"I wasn't thin enough," I said quickly. "I wasn't the perfect hostess for him. He controlled what I wore and how I acted and what I ate. He controlled *everything* about my life." I nibbled at my bottom lip. "That was why I left like I did, why I spent a long time looking over my shoulder. It was why—when he didn't come after me—I always figured that was why he didn't care about letting me go. That he'd found someone else to do it better than I ever could."

"Frankie, baby—"

"I haven't spoken to him in years." More nibbling. "But I'm sure that you know that, if you were looking into me for so long." I exhaled. "And I don't know why he was downstairs. He only said, *'We need to talk,'* and then you were barging in through the door and—"

His fingers flexed. "I'm sorry, baby."

"No," I said quickly. "I was scared. I was so glad you were there." Half of my mouth hitched up. "Though, of course, I didn't expect to be hauled off in handcuffs."

Another flex. Another apology in his eyes.

But there was a glimmer of lightness there too.

"I want to be with you," he said.

I blinked, having gone far beyond my question from a few moments before.

"I've wanted it for a long time, baby."

My eyes slid closed.

"And I think you're fucking perfect. Your body." His hand on my waist squeezed. "Your mind." He kissed my temple. "Your heart." His hand at my throat slid down, pressed to the spot there.

"I—"

But I didn't get any further words out because apparently, we were done talking.

He stood with me in his arms.

And he carried me to bed.

SEVENTEEN

LEX

The knock on my door had me looking up, seeing Cameron, Chance, and Carter—a fucking trio of C's—on my threshold, scowling at me.

Jesus.

Several of the Jacksons—Chance, Carter, and their father, Ben—had an open invitation to come to my work—and the clearance to manage it. Apparently, Cameron—a professional hockey player for the Oakland Eagles who was *not* typically found walking through the field offices located outside of Darlington—had either sweet-talked his way in or just relied on his brothers to clear the way.

Regardless of their methods, they were there.

Standing and glaring and ready to kick my ass.

Because we hadn't had our "talk" yet.

Mostly because I'd been busy.

And then had spent last night in Frankie's bed.

Not fucking her like I'd wanted. Just holding her, smelling the scent of her shampoo, understanding that we'd crossed some barriers but that others remained, that it would be easy to have sex—because, fuck, it had been good.

It was harder to lay there with my dick hard and my mind fully functional.

To think about what I'd done, what I was doing...and about the woman who I wanted to be mine.

I wanted walks on the beach in the middle of the night, wanted to come home and find her cackling with her friends. I wanted to hold her all night long, just like I had—holding her until her body went lax against mine, until her breathing went steady, until—

The door slammed shut and I blinked away those fantasies...

And stared up at the trio of angry C's who'd inundated my office.

Right. Our "talk."

I supposed I was lucky it was happening here in my office.

Where bloodshed likely wouldn't happen.

Though, they *had* closed the door.

I stood, leaned back against the corner of my desk, and braced, arms crossed.

"What the fuck?" Carter snapped. "Are you serious right now?"

Cameron glared but didn't reply.

Chance was the only one of them that didn't look like he was ready to murder me. He didn't look happy—don't get me wrong—he just didn't look like he was going to pull out the old tire iron and whack me across the kneecaps with it.

The better to let his brothers get their licks in.

"You guys know that I can't share information about actively open cases." Never mind that I'd divulged plenty to Frankie.

That was different.

She'd lived with that fucking monster, needed to understand enough to keep herself safe.

"This isn't information about an actively open case," Carter snapped. "This is you moving to Darlington with the sole purpose of fucking over a good woman."

Guilt rippled through me.

1. fucking-gain.

"I came to Darlington because Francis Lyon lives close and because you guys are here. I—"

"Bullshit."

"I *also*," I continued firmly, talking over him, "came here because Francis Lyon's daughter lived in Darlington and had ingratiated herself into *my* family and I had to make sure that she wasn't part of it."

"And you didn't trust that I would already have made the connections? Would have done the background checks when I found out my woman loved her?" Chance this time. A former agent. A smart man who now spent his time doing private investigation.

"Your wife know you investigated her friends?" I asked quietly.

A wince on Chance's face, but then his expression cleared, eyes narrowing. "I know how to get her to forgive me if she finds out. Would Frankie say the same for you?"

Now *I* was the one wincing.

She was being nice about it all.

Understanding even...when by rights she should be fucking *pissed*.

But she wasn't.

And why was that?

Why did it open up a pit in my stomach?

"Frankie and I have come to an understanding," I muttered.

Cameron snorted, shook his head.

Carter's expression wasn't much better. He glared at me. "I

thought I knew you, man. Thought that you were better than this."

Another blow.

More guilt.

"And I'll express exactly how fucking disappointed I am in you when we get into the ring at the gym."

Joy.

The fucking MMA gym that these bastards had talked me into joining.

And now they'd enjoy beating up on me.

All three of them at once—because the fuckers knew they couldn't take me one-on-one.

Though Cameron, with his hockey fighting skills...

"As much as I want to hand you your ass," Chance grumbled, "we haven't come here for that."

I raised my brows.

Chance didn't expound on that, just glanced over at Carter.

And that was when I noticed he had a laptop in his hands. The tension left me—or maybe, it just turned into a completely different type of tightness sitting like a rock in my stomach.

My stomach clenched. "What's up?"

Carter walked forward, settled the laptop on the corner of the desk. "We need help with a local case."

My gaze flicked to each of the brothers then back to the laptop.

Which Carter held steady as he opened the top.

That rock in my stomach turned into a boulder.

"Christ," I muttered. "What the fuck is that?"

Cam shook his head. "Candy."

I lifted my brows.

"A new street drug some of the kids in town have started using," he explained. "My former teammate is the hockey coach at the high school. He found some on the players, asked me to reach out to my brothers."

That explained Cam's odd mid-season visit home to his family.

I looked at Carter, who said, "We've been tracking this with the PD for a while. Though—until Cam brought it to our attention—we thought we'd managed to keep it out of the schools." A shake of his head. "Last weekend made it very clear we were wrong about that. Someone brought it to a party and gave it to all their friends."

Fuck.

"Unfortunately, the dumb fucks didn't realize it *wasn't* candy, that it was dangerous as hell," Carter said, clicking to the next screen. "It's fentanyl, and six of them ended up ODing."

Fuck.

"Anyone die?" I rasped.

"Luckily, no. The party was at one of our sheriff's houses. He got the SOS from his neighbors that shit was going down and called in a couple of squad cars." Carter shook his head. "Thankfully, they all had NARCAN in the medkits and an ambulance responded quickly for the others."

"Did they have enough for everyone?" I asked of the medication that could be used to treat overdoses quickly and effectively.

"Cleaned them all out," Carter muttered. "Now they're waiting for funding to approve more to come in and hoping to fuck that no one ODs in the meantime."

Jesus.

I made a note to talk to my boss, see if there were any resources for the local police departments to get more of the rescue medication, even if funding might be an issue. But there was more to this, I was sure of it. "And why are you three here now?" I asked, nodding toward the three C's.

"We've been working on shutting down this ring for a while," Chance said.

Okay.

I lifted my brows.

"And I went to your boss," Chance added. "She said you've got nothing but time"—a penetrating stare—"since you took yourself off the Lyon case."

More penetrating stares.

Three of them this time.

"I like Frankie," I muttered, giving a little in order to move the fuck on with this conversation. "Which means I leveled with her." I sighed. "It also means I'm too close to this to be an effective investigator. Attie and the others have worked this as long as me, and while I fucking hate sitting on the goddamned sidelines, I won't jeopardize the investigation. I told my boss that, she agreed to not fire my ass, so now I'm clearing the decks and then I'll start working on other cases."

Chance passed over a file folder and a flash drive.

"It *means* that you'll start working on *this* one."

EIGHTEEN

FRANKIE

I frowned as I pulled the box toward me, peeled back the flaps to peer inside...

And see yet another order I hadn't placed.

This time—my frown deepened—the contents were a supplement from a brand I didn't recognize. It was as weird as the delivery had been, crammed next to some empty boxes and bags of trash I needed to run to the dumpster, almost completely out of sight.

Normally my drivers came through the front door and left single boxes—like this one—on the counter, and if it was a delivery day, it was set up in advance because a significant amount of hauling everything back to my stock room was required.

Maybe he'd tried to come through the front?

I'd taken Lex's words to heart, not leaving the doors unlocked until Darlington woke up and I wasn't going to be taken by surprise by someone entering.

They could have tried the front, realized it was locked, and left the box by the back door, where they knew I would see it eventually.

Simple as that.

Or it could have been delivered to the wrong address.

I bent the flaps back in, studying the shipping label.

Nope.

It was made out to Earthly Delights.

And so I needed to make another phone call, make sure I wasn't being charged for something I hadn't ordered. Again.

Ugh.

I liked people. I loved helping them find their way to a healthier lifestyle, to products that made them feel better. I *didn't* love spending time on hold with customer service trying to make sure I wasn't nickeled and dimed into bankruptcy.

Tea first. And a snack.

Then I'd make the phone call, deal with all the outstanding admin that came from running a store, relieve my high schooler out front so she could actually go home and do things like see her family and eat dinner and finish her homework before midnight.

Only, after I'd shoved the box with the strange flower printed on the side and strode into the kitchen, I remembered I was out of tea.

Downstairs *and* upstairs.

I'd gone to make a cup this morning, bleary-eyed and feeling more than a little awkward with Lex taking up space in my apartment's kitchen and found the tin empty.

And the one down here had been thoroughly searched, the tea bags scattered on the floor and counter.

I hadn't tried to rescue them.

I'd just thrown them in the trash.

Sighing, I made a mental note to add an extra-large order when I called about the box that didn't belong and popped out into the front room to check on Kayla, my kickass high school kiddo.

Also, yes, I was putting off making the phone call.

"You good?" I asked after Kayla had finished ringing up one of our regulars.

"Good," Kayla said, closing the register. "We've been really busy, since you were closed for a couple of days." Pink on her cheeks. "Sorry, I—"

I squeezed her shoulder. "It's okay," I told her gently. "It's all figured out now."

Sort of.

Or at least, I wasn't anticipating being hauled off in hand-cuffs again.

"I'm glad."

I glanced toward the front windows, saw the sky was starting to darken, then back at her. "I just need to make a quick"—God, I hoped—"phone call, and then you can take off."

"Okay." She picked up the roll of hemp ribbon and a pair of scissors and my heart thumped.

I forced a smile, started to turn for the hall again.

"Oh, Frankie?"

I paused, glanced back. "Yeah, kiddo?"

"A man left this for you."

A man?

My heart thumped again, harder this time, but I stepped toward the bag. Probably, I should have stopped, called Lex, but I reached for the note taped to the outside of the nondescript brown bag and unfolded it anyway, read through the masculine scrawl.

Saw you were out.
-L

I inhaled, pulled the paper from the inside and peered into the bag.

And then felt my heart thump for a third time.

A tin of tea—*my* tea—was inside.

I exhaled.

Then I slipped back into the kitchen, made myself a cup...

And *then* I called customer service.

———

Eventually, night fell and I closed up shop. I went upstairs, was sitting on my couch, a book open in my lap, contemplating dinner but delaying making it because—

A knock at the door.

Because of *that*.

I'd been expecting that knock.

It was late, well past when I would normally eat, but it wasn't unheard of when I ran a cooking class.

But tonight there hadn't been any classes.

I glanced at my phone, saw the motion notice from my newly installed doorbell, and clicked it, my belly going warm at the sight of Lex's big body standing outside my door, his gaze on the camera.

He knew it was there.

He'd installed it the same morning I found the shop cleaned.

But also...he'd helped me set up the app this morning.

And now, I had him on my phone, looking at the camera, waiting for me to let him in.

God, this was something I'd wanted for so long.

A fantasy. A dream. Something that would never be.

Only, it was.

I dropped my cell on the coffee table, set my book face down on the arm of the couch, and got up, moving through the small space, gripping the handle, my belly full of flutters.

And then the door was open, and he was moving in, forcing me back because he was big and the space was small, but not forcing me back for long because as soon as he was in and the door closed and locked, his arm had gone around my middle.

A heartbeat later, I was against his chest, pulse pounding, my senses filled with *him*.

At least until his stomach rumbled.

His arms tightened when I started to pull back, but I kept moving, and though he put up a sliver of resistance, he eventually let me shift away from him enough to meet his gaze. "Pesto pasta or chicken salad?"

He groaned. "Killing me, baby."

My lips curved.

Because I'd pulled out the big guns.

I knew he liked both of those that I made on the regular.

Pretty much everyone in our circle loved them.

"Or," I said, tugging away from the circle of his arms and going to the fridge. "You can put some chicken salad on some greens for an appetizer, and I start the pasta."

He caught me before I could open the fridge door, stepping close, pinning me between his body and the cool metal. "Baby."

My heart was pounding. Because I liked the hold, liked the show of strength, liked the way he felt pressed to my back.

Loved it really.

"What's wrong?"

His hand settled on my shoulder, and he leaned back enough to trail it down my body. "I'm supposed to take you to dinner."

"I-I like cooking."

He was silent, hand slowly trailing up and down. "I promised you dinner and haven't taken you yet."

"It's been pretty busy."

"Yeah."

That had me turning around. Because it sounded wrong. "It'll hold," I told him. "And it's late, so I'll cook tonight." My lips tipped up. "You can take me for pancakes at the diner in the morning."

I expected him to smile back. Instead, he looked...troubled.

I lifted a hand, touched his cheek. "What is it?"

"You're trying to take care of me."

I nibbled at my lip. "It's just cooking dinner." A beat. "It's nothing." I brushed my fingers along his jaw. "Really, baby."

"Chance is right," he muttered.

"What?"

"And I don't get it either."

My brows dragged together. "Get what?"

"How you're not pissed at me."

Nineteen

S urprise across her face.

Deep pools of emerald on mine.

Heavy, almost oppressive silence.

Then she spoke, and it wasn't anything like the Frankie I'd come to know since I'd moved to Darlington.

It was soft and gentle and vulnerable...but it was also jaded.

Hurt.

Because she had been.

"I'm used to it."

"Used to what?" I asked carefully, my intestines twisting, knowing that this wasn't going to be something I liked.

Knowing it was going slice my insides to ribbons.

"Men treating me like shit," she said, her chin coming up. A shrug, something different growing in her expression. Steel. *Fire.* That I liked. I hated the hurt, but I was so fucking proud of her for the way her chin lifted and her shoulders straightened. Strong. So *fucking* strong. "I grew up with it. I got *used* to it." A laugh that wasn't the least bit amused. "You know why I have a health shop?"

I knew a lot of things about Francesa Lyon.

But I didn't know that.

"You know I had that team of people taking care of me when I was growing up."

I nodded. Braced. Waited.

"I had more etiquette lessons than actual schoolwork, and a personal trainer and a dietician and a chef and a stylist and a makeup artist and an esthetician and a hairdresser from the moment I turned ten. Because I couldn't be a Lyon and not be made presentable. Because—God forbid—I gained a few pounds or showed up at an event with a pimple that wasn't properly covered or eye shadow that clashed with my outfit. God forbid, I did anything that wasn't going to make my father proud."

My lungs felt like they were going to explode.

"Eventually, though," she whispered. "It was too much."

"Baby."

"It was too much, and I stopped eating anything that wasn't explicitly put in front of me. I stopped having opinions about my hair and makeup and clothes. I stopped complaining about the workouts." She sighed. "I stopped being myself. I stopped being anything but that facsimile of a person that was my father's image."

"*Baby.*"

Her hands clenched into fists. "And it wasn't good enough. Not when I was under a hundred pounds and made up like a doll. Not when I was smiling and serving drinks in clothes that stole my ability to breathe and shoes that killed my feet. Not when I was doing every single thing he asked of me." A beat. "And more. And then one day I looked in the mirror and I *hated* myself. Someone had brought me breakfast, and I couldn't stomach a bite. I studied my reflection and I didn't have a single strand of hair that was out of place, not one eyelash that was left uncurled or uncoated with mascara. My outfit was perfect, my heels expensive. And I could not live *one* more second in my life, my body, that house."

An exhale, those hands relaxing.

I took one in mine, held it against my chest.

"So...I left." She pressed her lips flat. "I don't know where I got the strength. Or if it was just that urgency to not be in my own skin, but that night when my dad flew out, I just...left." She shook her head. "Only the memories didn't leave so easily. I didn't eat normally for years and I couldn't—*can't*—look in the mirror and not still see every flaw."

My heart convulsed.

Fuck.

"You're beautiful, baby."

They weren't the right words, probably. Certainly, they weren't *all* the words she needed to hear.

But I had to make sure she knew that much.

The ice around her thawed, eyes softening. "I'm working on seeing it." Her mouth curved. "Of course, it's easier to get someone else to see it in themselves than believe it myself."

I touched her cheek.

"So, I'm working on loving myself, but..." A sigh that was so fucking sad I wanted to put my fist through the wall. "But I'm not used to anyone else loving me."

"Your friends."

She nodded, eyes glimmering. "You're right, of course. We love each other." Her eyes slid to the side. "But it's not the same as a parent's love, is it? Not the same as a partner's."

She was right.

It wasn't.

"No, baby, it's not."

"So..." A breath. "The truth is that I'm used to it—to being forgotten and an afterthought, and I'm used to being *used*." She shook her head. "It sounds fucking awful, doesn't it? Like I'm some weak ass doormat who's willing to accept a man treating me like shit just because I had a traumatic childhood."

God, my fucking heart *hurt* for her. "Baby."

"I don't accept it," she whispered. "I don't accept *it.*" A sigh. "But I get it. I understand what you thought and why you thought it, and I don't hold it against you. Not really." A breath. "I hate that people in town saw that, hate that I don't know what they think. But they showed up today. They bought products they love or that improve their lives or that just...taste good. They made a point to come, to show me that nothing's changed."

Of course they did.

Because this town was fucking perfect.

Except for a new street drug that was causing kids to overdose.

But that wasn't something I could think about right then, not with Frankie's eyes glimmering and her shoulders straight, her chin up.

Consciously, I knew there were different kinds of strength in our world—the brute, physical strength I had, the bold strength that was Attie and her abilities at the bureau, the gentle, resilient strength of Raven as she cared for people in the emergency department.

But now I understood the quiet strength that was Frankie.

She was sweet and soft and kind.

But...that didn't mean she wasn't equally as powerful.

"So, I can forgive you for what you did." A shrug. "Because you're trying to help the world and because while it was scary and heart-wrenching, ultimately my store will be okay and I've learned things about my father that I need to know, and..." She shook her head. "I know I'll be okay. Because I've survived more, because I've thrived, because I've left a man who wasn't good for me." Her eyes locked with mine, held, sending me a message that

I couldn't miss, that was reinforced when she added, "Because I can do it again."

I would have smiled if I didn't want to kiss her senseless.

Because...message received.

Same as the message in my heart that had been received by my brain—

She's mine.

It was as simple as that.

I'd been fighting it. Ignoring it. Trying to sabotage it.

But if I'd held on to a sliver of doubt before this conversation, her words would have made that disappear like so much smoke.

The wind picked up.

And...poof.

Any slender filaments of doubt were gone.

"I know you can, baby," I murmured. "Because you're one of the strongest people I've ever met."

Her eyes went wide, but I was already bending, already lifting her in my arms, striding toward the couch.

I deposited her on the cushions.

"Read," I ordered softly when she stared up at me with wide eyes. "*I'll* cook us dinner."

TWENTY

FRANKIE

I couldn't believe I'd told him all of that.

I couldn't believe he hadn't gotten pissed and stormed off and turned it into something else. I couldn't believe—

"*Ack!*" I squealed as he bent and lifted me up in a smooth movement, hauling me against his chest, carrying me across the room, settling me on the couch.

"Read," he ordered softly. "I'll cook us dinner."

I inhaled sharply. "Lex."

Fingers on my cheek. "I've watched you read until you fell asleep countless times."

My brows shot up. "Y-you have?"

He nodded toward the window that took up a good portion of my front room. The window that faced *his* window. "I watched you read and eat and sleep and hang with your friends. I watched you drink tea"—my heart pulsed, remembering the tin of tea he'd left for me earlier that day—"and I watched you be Frankie far more than I really could justify for the case, far more than I wanted to admit."

"I—" I pressed my lips flat, released them. "I don't know what to say."

He cupped my jaw, eyes starting to sparkle with humor. "You could say I'm a goddamned creeper." His hand flexed. "And it would be true. Because I drained the batteries in my night vision binoculars enough fucking times that I should have known I was being an idiot."

"You did?"

He nodded. "Yeah, baby, I did."

"But why? I mean"—I shrugged—"I know it was the case but that seems…"

"Obsessive? Like I was fighting in the inevitable?"

"Um…yeah," I whispered. "Emphasis on the obsessive."

He chuckled, and hell, if I didn't feel that between my legs. "Definitely obsessive, but all of those hours watching through the windows can't compare to ten minutes in your presence, baby," he murmured. "It didn't tell me what your body feels like against mine or give me the soft scent of your shampoo. I couldn't count the freckles on your nose or see the exact shade of pink your cheeks turn when I kiss you."

"But you spent time with me before," I whispered. "When we had dinner at Misty's or Raven's or at Mr. and Mrs. Jackson's place. We've spent lots of time together over the last year. You even—"

He'd even come here once before.

When he'd acted like a jerk and apologized.

"I was pretty torn up, baby," he murmured. "I told you about Hailey and I swear to fuck, one second I was sure you were exactly like her, and the next, I was convinced you were a fucking saint."

My inhale was long and deep.

That explained…a lot.

How he'd be really cool one moment and then snap the next —though, he'd only truly crossed the line one time.

The others had just felt like he'd erected a wall—like one second, he was with me...and the next, he stood on the other side of the Grand Canyon.

"You're not like Hailey," he murmured. "You're not your father. You're just Frankie and I've learned that *just Frankie* is fucking incredible."

My heart squeezed again, and I reached up, touched his cheek. "Can we just...put the past aside and move on from here?"

I didn't like the guilt in his eyes.

"No."

I blinked.

"No fucking way," he said, hand covering mine, pressing my palm against the stubble on his cheek. "No way are we going back. No way am I forgetting," he vowed—and, yes, it was a vow, one I felt in the depths of my soul. "No way am I going back."

"But—"

He stayed close, eyes on mine. "But what, baby?"

I had a choice here.

I could be the old me, content to sit and wait to soak in whatever scraps of sunshine shone my way.

Or...I could be *me*.

I could seize my life by both hands, could start living how I wanted to live. I could take what I wanted.

And I'd wanted Lex—a man like Lex—for as long as I could remember.

Warm eyes, gentle touches, honestly that may not be the prettiest, but *was* honest.

That was the future I wanted.

That was the future I was desperate for.

So, I lifted my chin. "But how can I be sure that you won't change your mind again?" I exhaled, kept going. "How can I be sure that your past won't crop up again and I'll suffer for it?

How can I be *sure* that you'll still want me even when shit gets real?"

He was silent for long enough that I began to lose my spine.

But he didn't lift his hand, didn't pull back from me.

"I don't think you can *ever* be one hundred percent sure, baby," he murmured. "But I believe in what I feel for you enough that I stepped back from a case I worked years for because I know that I can't have that *and* you. And once I really allowed myself to see you, I knew I'd never really wanted anything else."

I sucked in a breath, heart pounding so hard and fast that I felt it in the back of my throat.

And all I managed to come up with to say back was, "Oh."

He grinned. "Yeah. *Oh.* "

Only then did he slip his hand from mine.

Only then did he straighten and move to the kitchen.

Only then did he casually toss over his shoulder after surveying the contents of my fridge, "Now, baby. Grilled cheese sandwiches or burgers?"

"I—"

He waited, not impatient, not frustrated as I worked through the whirlwind in my head, worked through all he'd told me and, ultimately, all I knew, deep down, that I wanted.

And it wasn't to make a choice between hamburgers and grilled cheese sandwiches.

He waited as I crossed to him, as I shored up my courage and reached for what I really wanted. "How about you cook for me another time?"

A cloud across his expression. "Baby," he warned.

"Because"—I reached behind him, tugged open the fridge, pulled out the glass container of chicken salad, then moved to the drawer, pulled out two forks—"we can eat *this* in bed."

One second, he was standing there, those storm clouds on his face.

The next, he was moving toward me, scooping me up again. Only this time, he was carrying me to my bed instead of the couch. We tumbled onto the mattress, his big body taking the bulk of the impact while I managed to keep hold of the forks and container.

I was stunned by the turn of events, but...I was going with it.

Which was why I just curled up against him when he reclined against the headboard with me in his arms, opened the glass container, and...

Then we ate chicken salad.

But instead of both of us each using our own fork...

We shared.

TWENTY-ONE

LEX

I'd expected her to tell me to leave.

And now I was in her bed.

Which was infinitely better with sheets and a bedspread and pillows with cases.

Which...had me feeling like an asshole again.

But I tucked the feeling deep, held it tight. Logically, I understood my actions. But logic didn't play. I didn't like feeling like an asshole, didn't like that I'd made her feel bad, so I wasn't tucking it away to move on.

I was holding on to it so I wouldn't forget.

Months of pretending she was something else even though I knew different.

Years of letting my fuckups from the past sit heavy on my heart and affect the man I was.

Yeah, there wouldn't just be moving forward.

But I wouldn't go back either.

Which was why I'd returned the container to the kitchen, retrieved Frankie's book, and was blatantly watching her as she turned page after page...interspersed with glances up at me and pink cheeks and shifting hips.

Which was when I started noticing more.

Those pages turning more slowly.

Those pinks growing deeper, brighter.

Those hips moving more frequently.

Her eyes came to mine again, dark green emeralds that were on fire.

Those cheeks went fire engine red.

The pieces in my mind finally clicked into place. "What are you reading, baby?"

The book was clamped closed and she avoided my eyes. "Are you just going to watch me all night?"

I shrugged, as well as I was able to, anyway, considering I was reclined on the bed with this woman in my arms—which was to say, not very well. "Best view I've ever had."

Those cheeks flared again, her fingers tightening on the book, reminding me—

I snagged the paperback from her hands, flipped it over so I could see the cover...

It looked innocuous, a simple carton cityscape on the front, so I flipped to the back.

"What are you—?"

I nudged her fingers away when she tried to snag it from me, my eyes trailing over the description of a tough cowboy falling for the woman of his dreams.

"Lex," she began.

"Do I need to get a cowboy hat?"

She groaned, buried her face in my chest. "Seriously?"

I took that opportunity to start flipping through the pages of the book—toward the back, where she'd been doing that glancing up and blushing and hip writhing—

"*Oh,*" I said as the words penetrated—

Penetrated.

Which was not right the word to be crossing through my mind cuddled up next to Frankie as she'd—apparently—been reading about a woman who was being thoroughly...*penetrated*.

Her head shot up, gaze going to my hands and then my face, my brows still nearly at my hairline.

Those cheeks somehow went even more red and then she was moving, snatching at the book.

No fucking way.

I rolled to my back, eyes scanning the page as I kept it out of her reach. "Jesus, baby, I know that you're fucking incredible in bed, but do you really want me to put my dick—"

She clambered on top of me in a flash, legs straddling my middle, sending the air from my lungs.

Since I had lost my breath *and* now had a gorgeous woman on top of me, I became much less focused on the book.

She snagged it, sent it sailing across the room, breathing heavily as she shoved her hair out of her face.

"Don't—" she warned.

I dropped my hands to her hips. "Don't think about how much I want to do that to you?" I said, squeezing lightly, allowing my fingers to dip beneath the waistband of her pajama pants. She shivered, hips jerking. "Or don't think about how I wish you were naked *while* you were on top of me right now?"

She froze, seemed to recognize her position.

Our eyes locked.

Heat seemed to shimmer in the air between us.

And then, proving that she was fire-forged steel beneath that soft exterior, she reached for the hem of her shirt.

And ripped it up over her head.

No bra.

That was thought one.

And that was the *last* thought before I reacted on instinct—flipping us, pinning her to the mattress. I arched, bending down so I could take her nipple in my mouth.

She gasped as I rolled the taut bud on my tongue, hands diving into my hair, keeping me against her.

I groaned when her nails bit into my scalp.

My cock ached, pushed against the zipper on my jeans as she arched against me.

Gentle, I needed to be gentle.

But I was afraid I wasn't very much so as I shoved my hand into her pajamas, dragged my finger through her slick folds, pressed at her clit.

She gasped again, arched against me. "Lex!"

Yeah, not gentle.

I couldn't be gentle.

And, I realized dimly in the back of my caveman brain, that she didn't want that either. Not as those nails scored lines down my back, not as she forced them into the backs of my jeans, gripping my ass as she ground up against me. Not as she groaned my name and tried to find purchase against my fingers—

I slid one deep inside.

Her pussy rippled, clenched.

Yeah, I liked that, a whole fucking lot.

So much so that I slid another finger in, that I reveled in the clench of it around me.

So much so that I pushed another inside—

She shuddered. "Oh fuck! I—"

I bent and sucked her nipple deep, drawing on it in rhythm to the strokes of my fingers fucking her tight cunt—slow and steady and rough. I felt her close in on an orgasm, felt it in the shivers wracking her body, the way her pussy rippled around my fingers. I felt it in the heat of her skin and the sheen of sweat on her forehead.

I felt it in her moans as they vibrated through her chest, as they danced along my tongue.

And then...

It was *there.*

She was coming apart on my fingers and tongue, my name in the air, her body going so fucking tense and—

Then slumping back onto the mattress, body going limp.

I stroked into the slick heat of her a few more times, not wanting to let that pussy go, not wanting to slip out and break the connection.

Her eyes peeled open.

Slowly.

Hazy green irises.

I lifted my head, kissed a slow path up to her throat, along her jaw, her cheek, leaning in to brush her nose with my own. Her eyes closed, and she wrapped an arm around me, cuddling close.

Only then did I withdraw my fingers, loving the way her mouth formed a silent protest.

I kissed her lightly, asked,

"Should I go get your book, so you can read before you go to sleep, baby?"

TWENTY-TWO

FRANKIE

My mind was thoroughly focused on this man, on what he'd just done to my body.

On the fact that I'd never come as fast or as hard.

On his hard cock pulsing against my thigh.

So why the hell was he talking about books?

My book?

I blinked, shook myself.

He'd made me come like *that* and now he expected me to just casually crawl back into his arms and read like I wasn't being wracked with aftershocks of pleasure.

Like I didn't want him inside me?

He started to get out of bed, apparently intent on retrieving my spicy romance.

That wasn't going to work for me.

Which was why I caught his arm and—oh, look at that—my fingers went to the waistband of his jeans...and flicked them open.

And—*oh, look at that*—his zipper just slid right down.

"Frankie, baby—" he rasped as his cock sprang free.

I grinned up at him, noting that he wasn't fighting me too hard as I wrapped my hand around him, as I pumped once, twice.

"I don't want my book," I murmured. "I want you inside me again."

"Baby," he said. "We rushed before and—"

God, I *liked* him.

I sat up, released him, not wanting to, but also knowing it was a necessary evil because I needed to push off my pants.

Because I needed to reenact that scene I'd been reading.

I stood, my pajama pants, my underwear falling to the floor, and stepped out of them.

He sucked in a breath—and yeah, I liked that.

Yeah, that made me feel fucking great.

I bent, pressed my front to the bed, leaving my ass in the air, and spread my legs. "I was kind of thinking about skipping the reading part and moving right toward the acting it out in real life portion of events."

He inhaled sharply again.

I looked over my shoulder, taking in the sight of him so big and strong, his hard cock jutting out, and I licked my lips.

"Fuck," he growled.

And then he was moving, reaching into his back pocket and pulling out a condom—tearing it open with his teeth, rolling it over the hard length of his cock. He shoved his boxer briefs down, stepped out of his jeans.

Then his palm landed between my shoulder blades.

"What'd you want to act out, baby?" he rasped. "Me holding you down while I fuck you senseless?"

I had a full body shiver.

"Or," he went on. "Me picking you up so you're on all fours

and driving into you again"—his hand slid down, dipped between my legs—"and *again?*"

Another shiver.

"Or should I lick that pussy of yours—lick it until you're begging for my cock."

I inhaled. Exhaled.

"Yes."

His fingers came to my chin, his other hand was between my legs. "To which one, baby?"

"Yes," I said again because that hand between my legs was— "Oh, God," I whispered.

He chuckled, and—thank fuck—he stopped asking me questions.

His fingers got to work.

And then his mouth.

And then his cock.

And my *yes* got me all of those fantasies, all of him.

Including being held close afterward, his big, strong body wrapped around mine, his fingers running along my naked skin, tracing nonsensical patterns as we talked about our days. When I yawned, though, I felt something in him change, an urgency in his body, his touch, his words.

"I really am sorry," he said, like he was desperate for me to understand how much he meant it.

I stroked a hand through his hair. "I know," I told him, wanting him to know that I did get it. "And I really do want to forget about it and explore what we have between us."

His big body tensed, but he was beyond gentle when he cupped my jaw, tilted my head up so our stares locked. "And I really won't forget what I did in the name of fear."

I released a breath, those words settling deep.

But before I could reply, he kept talking. "I won't forget. I won't forget because you deserve better." A brush of his mouth over mine.

Then he shifted us, settling me against his chest.

And he held me tight.

Just before I drifted off to sleep, he asked, "Can I cook you dinner tomorrow night?"

My mouth curved.

"I'd like that," I whispered. "So long as you let me make you dessert."

His arms tightened, and he pressed a kiss to the top of my head. "Deal."

His rough chuckle was the last thing I heard before I fell asleep.

———

Buzzing woke me what felt like minutes later.

And the mattress shifted, bouncing me against a hard chest.

Groggy, I peeled open my eyes, watched as Lex reached behind him and snagged his phone from the nightstand. "'lo?" he rumbled. "This is Agent Blackwell."

He paused, clearly listening, then began talking again, his rough, sleep-laced voice filling my senses as it radiated through his chest, filled my ears. I smiled, liking the sound of him so close, liking him in my bed even more, and started to slide back off to sleep.

But then his body went from relaxed to tense in a millisecond.

My eyes flew back open, and I lifted up enough to see his face.

The expression there had my gut twisting.

He noticed—because of course he did. "Not your dad," he murmured, instantly settling me. Then into the phone, "I'll be there in twenty."

I exhaled, nodded, and followed him when he got out of bed, still talking on his cell. I moved to my coffee maker, knowing that he'd probably need the caffeine. It wasn't as healthy as my tea, but I believed in living healthy, not with restrictions. I indulged on occasion, and I just made sure that I did it with organic beans that were grown in humane conditions.

Plus, my tea wasn't caffeine-free, so I had no high horse to preach from.

He was still talking as he dressed, as I let the coffee brew and I filled a carafe with coffee and a dash of milk—no sugar.

He was talking as he came to me, wrapping an arm around my waist, kissing the top of my head again in that gentle way that made my heart squeeze, that had his big, warm body surrounding me, that brought his scent to my nose.

"Yeah," he said into the phone. "I'm leaving now."

I held up the to-go cup, got a sweet and sexy smile in return.

"Thanks, baby," he murmured, pinning his cell between shoulder and ear and taking it from me, not dropping the hand from around my waist as he moved to the door. I went with him, not because he forced me—though I easily could have been dragged along because he was so much bigger and stronger than me—but because his hold was gentle and I wanted to be in the circle of his arm and...walking him to the door felt like the most natural thing ever.

He only dropped his arm after he'd kissed me lightly on the lips, ordering me softly to, "Lock up."

I nodded, waving as he pounded down the exterior stairs. I turned, starting to move back into my apartment, but something caught my eye and I paused, frowned, and bent...

To pick up an envelope that had been propped near my planter.

My frown didn't ease when I came back inside and saw my name in the front.

Nor when I set it on the counter and debated what to do.

I should call Lex.

But he was on the other line and clearly heading off to something critically important.

So...I did nothing, just left it on the counter to deal with later.

That was the wrong call—but not something I would understand until *later*. Much, much later.

But I didn't know how important it was then, so all I did was lock the door.

And then crawl back into a bed that smelled of all my hopes and dreams.

Twenty-Three

LEX

There was something about the hours of two to four in the morning that made it ripe for crime.

Darkness for cover.

The world sleeping, especially in a small town like Darlington.

This wasn't New York City or Las Vegas.

The roads rolled up at ten at night...if people even made it that late.

So that I was driving through town to the high school parking lot at this fucking hour didn't bode good things.

That I'd been called in by my boss—and then Carter when I was halfway there—was also not good.

That I pulled up on the scene to see it secured with yellow police tape and occupied by no less than a half-dozen squad cars and several unmarked vehicles sent my stomach twisting. Especially, when mine wasn't the only civilian car there.

I pulled next to another SUV, got out, and immediately

spotted Carter, flashing my badge as I slipped under the tape, moved toward him.

The sick look on his face told me enough.

"What happened?"

He shoved the notebook he'd been writing on in his pocket, shook his head. "Neighbor woke up to what they thought were fireworks."

"Gunshots?"

A nod. "They got out of bed, saw the flashes, realized it wasn't fireworks after all. Called the police." He sighed. "I happened to be coming back from a late stakeout, and I..." His head swiveled and I watched him go somewhere else, go back to the place where it wasn't healthy.

"Carter," I said quietly.

He glanced back at me, a muscle in flickering in his jaw.

"We both know it doesn't get easier," I said, still quiet. "To see this shit," I added when he didn't reply.

His jaw went even more tense.

"But you and Chance are doing something about."

He exhaled. "Yeah," he muttered.

"So," I said, deliberately changing the subject. "What did you find?"

"Two deceased when I made it onto the scene," he said quietly. "I secured the area, radioed the station for backup."

"Gunshots?"

A nod. "Yeah. Right through the head. No chance of survival." A breath. "But I found Candy on scene—" He dug out his phone, showed me a series of pictures I knew I wouldn't be able to unsee, but also that he needed to show me. "I can't be sure it wasn't planted to throw us off the trail," he said, pausing on a picture of the two deceased along with a smattering of drugs surrounding them, "or if it was a deal gone wrong."

Yeah, I got what he meant.

Obviously, there were drugs on scene, easily spotted in the

photos Carter had snapped, that the crime scene team was documenting with flashes of their high-res cameras, but I agreed with Carter. I couldn't be certain they hadn't been planted or if this was a drug deal that had turned bad.

Something about the way they were scattered spoke of things not being what they seemed.

But there also weren't a lot of reasons—outside of drugs—that people ended up dead.

"They'll run a tox screen," I told him. "We'll have more information then." Because we'd find out if they had drugs in their systems, if they had signs of chronic use. "Any ID on them?"

"CSI is going to retrieve their wallets, if they have them," Carter said shifting and putting his phone away, eyes going back to the blocked-off area where the crew was working. "But I recognize the bigger one. His name is Mack Villahue. He's been popped for some petty shit, breaking and entering, drunk and disorderly. But nothing to do with drugs—at least not that I'm aware of."

I nodded, not liking this the more information I had.

Not liking that two people had ended up dead for something that would never be able to be justified—it never was when shit like this went down.

Definitely not liking that this had all taken place in the parking lot of the local high school.

But, most of all, not liking that this was happening along a very particular modus operandi—one I was familiar with.

Because it was a page out of the Francis Lyon drug playbook.

Plant the dealers, the drugs in the community, make sure there was enough to really get it circulating.

Get people hooked.

And that was when the money would start flowing.

Lyon would be happy, people's lives would be fucked up, and he'd expand his trade of both women and flesh and substances that messed with the peace of the surrounding community.

Darlington was supposed to be a simple small town—that explosion of Hallmark magic.

Drugs and double homicides took the shine right off that.

"We need to watch out for—" What was going to be my warning to Carter about this being too fucking much of a coincidence to *not* involve Lyon cut off when I caught a flash out of the corner of my eye.

Not the cameras.

But...movement in the bushes.

Carter seemed to clock it at the same time I did—head whipping toward the spot I'd focused in on, hand going to his gun at his hip. He glanced at me and I nodded, trailing him when he started to move forward, to the bushes, boots clipping on the ground as he went.

He slowed as he approached the swathe of branches, the dark green leaves nearly black in this corner of the parking lot.

All of the lights were pointed the other direction.

He unclipped his flashlight, flicked it on.

The bushes rustled again.

I braced, my own gun out of its holster, down at my side, finger resting on the barrel above the trigger.

On alert.

Ready.

But not about to shoot someone if things got a little jumpy.

Carter pointed the stream of light into the bushes, and I caught another glimpse of movement. It was white—like a T-shirt or...

Skin.

Like pale skin that hadn't seen sunshine in a long, long time.

Even as that was processing and I was moving forward, returning my gun to the holster, Carter was doing the same, only faster because he was closer and had a clearer view and—

The flashlight hit the ground, stream of light bouncing this way and that until it landed, pointing right toward the source of movement.

Carter dropped to his knees, pushed the branches of the bushes out of the way.

And revealed...

"Fuck," I growled, turning back toward the group of squad cars, voice raising, "Call an ambulance. Right fucking now!"

Because it was a woman who'd apparently been tossed into the bushes.

Tossed because there was no fucking way she would have been able to run or walk or even, *crawl*, considering how beat to shit she was.

Tossed because there were branches protruding from her body.

Tossed because she was barely conscious.

Tossed because—

Fucking hell, she was barely alive.

Twenty-Four

Frankie

The scent of cooking filled my small kitchen.

Why was it not a surprise that the man was a good cook?

Some sort of vegetable soup simmered on my stove, there was bread in the oven, and wine in my glass.

The best part of all?

A barefoot, jeans-clad, tight T-shirt wearing Lex owning my kitchen like he'd been born and raised there.

"Are you sure I can't help?" I asked softly.

He'd been in the middle of lifting a wooden spoon to his lips, mouth pursed as he blew on the hot liquid.

The look he shot me was hot and commanding.

And clearly stated, *No.*

"Okay," I said, raising my hands, one palm flat out, the other holding my glass of organic wine. "I'll just sit here and watch my show."

Ostensibly, it was to watch the crappy reality show that

Misty had gotten us all addicted to years ago. In reality, my show was watching Lex in the kitchen. Why was it so hot watching a man cook?

I didn't know.

I also didn't *care* to know.

Because he *was* hot and he'd made me fresh-baked bread. From scratch—like legit with yeast and proofing and unbleached flour.

Yup, the man kept proving that he knew me.

And sitting here, watching my *show*, and I was content with how things had worked out.

Okay, I was *thrilled* with how things worked out.

My dreams. My fantasies. My life as I'd always wanted it.

Not a mansion. Not fancy clothes and caviar and a person to do my hair and makeup every day. Not so skinny that I could count every single one of my ribs. Not miserable and trapped and quiet, so fucking quiet I almost forgot the sound of my own voice.

With a man who knew I preferred to use unbleached flour.

And my brand of tea.

And that I'd been teaching a cooking class that afternoon—one that had run into the early evening, so he hadn't called, had just popped into the kitchen at Earthly Delights, teased a kiss out of me, much to the delight of all of my patrons (and something I knew would be all over town before the sun set), then had come upstairs and started cooking for me.

For *me*.

My heart rolled over in my chest.

Before my father had shown up in my shop and my world had imploded, it was everything I'd dreamed of.

Now...I knew my dreams didn't come close to what I *could* have.

If I kept having courage, kept standing up for myself, kept reaching for those dreams.

No more quiet, small Frankie.

I was the kickass owner of Earthly Delights. I'd fought through my past and built a good life. I could have the life I wanted.

My heart was pounding and my eyes stung, but I'd gone a few days without tears and I was determined to continue building that streak. More fantasies becoming reality. More dreams. More of that big, sexy man in my kitchen.

Giving me a show.

A strip of skin appeared above the waistband of his jeans as he bent to check on the bread, pulling open the oven door and probing at the loaf, giving me a peekaboo of the muscles I'd dug my nails into. Marks I could still see the edges of when his shirt slid up further.

Bright red tracks that had me glancing away, feeling more than a little guilty.

"What's with the face, baby?"

I hadn't even heard him move, but then he was in front of me, his hand taking mine, slipping the glass free and setting it on the coffee table. "I hurt you," I murmured.

His brows dragged together.

"You have my nail marks on your back," I explained.

Now his expression cleared, and went...*wolfish.* "I like— really like—what got me those nail marks."

I inhaled.

My pussy went wet.

His mouth stole mine in a kiss that left me breathless when he backed away, when he straightened and handed me my wine again. "Promise me you'll do it again," he murmured silkily, hand sliding up my thigh, warm and broad and *hot* as it settled right near the motherland. "Promise me you'll do it *tonight.*"

I inhaled sharply, and nearly spilled my wine.

He grinned that sexy grin, pulled his hand back.

Then returned to the kitchen. The bread came out of the

oven. The soup was turned off. Bowls were retrieved. Spoons and napkins set out.

While I breathed and tried not to jump him.

Then I decided if I was trying to be good and *not* jump him then I could at least give in to the urge to be closer to him.

I pushed up from the couch, moved to the counter, hopping up on the edge and scattering my mail I'd tossed there earlier. "Will you tell me about your family?"

He froze, the ladle he'd been using to scoop up soup freezing in turn. "What do you want to know?" he asked carefully.

Carefully.

Not coldly. Not pushing me away.

But definitely a wall up there.

"I mean...I don't really know anything about you." Which wasn't fair. "Other than the story of you and your two other Musketeers and the trouble you caused."

Now his face gentled. "The story's not super exciting. My dad died when I was young. My mom worked a lot, wasn't much interested in being a parent outside of making sure I had a roof over my head. I spent more time with the Jacksons than I did her." He sighed, commenced ladling and then turned out the bread onto a cutting board. "In fact, it was almost a relief when she passed away a few years ago. No more obligatory calls or visits. No more pretending that we were close when we weren't."

"I'm sorry," I murmured, reaching for his hand when he turned back toward me, drawing him close.

He shrugged. "It is what it is, and I was lucky that the Jacksons were in my life. I never really felt the loss of either parent."

I didn't think that was true.

I also didn't think it was a good sign that he'd had Hailey in his life, who'd lied and manipulated him, *and* a mother who'd failed him. Two important women in his past who hadn't stepped up, who'd hurt him, no matter what he said now.

I opened my mouth to say...something, but I didn't get the chance to because he had come close again, his hand settling near my thigh. "Baby, I—" He froze, glanced down. "What is this?"

I looked, saw that weird envelope I'd brought in early that morning.

I'd forgotten all about it with the whirlwind of the day, but there it was, sitting right beneath the mail I'd dumped there before the cooking class.

I picked it up, handed it to him. "I found it on the porch when you left this morning—"

He tore open the flap, brows snapping down as he pulled out the paper inside and began reading it.

I felt his temper rippled through the air.

"This shit"—he waved the envelope in my face—"is from your father! I thought I made it clear that we don't fuck around with things that are involving him. You need to be smart and careful and—"

I hopped down from the counter, plunked my hands on my hips. "First of all, I didn't *know* it was from him," I snapped. "I thought it was weird and that was why I didn't open it. I was going to tell you, but you were off somewhere in a hurry, somewhere that was clearly important. It wasn't a bomb. It's a letter and we could deal with it later. And," I went on, still snapping when he started to argue back, "I had a busy freaking day and it slipped my mind, but clearly I wasn't trying to hide it." I snatched it from him and dropped it on the counter, where it had been living since that morning. "It was right there and you were in my apartment by yourself. You could have seen it at any point."

He narrowed his eyes. "In the future," he gritted out, "if you get *anything* weird on your porch, if your instincts are pricked even the slightest bit then you should tell me. Immediately." A beat. "Even if it's two-fucking-thirty in the morning."

I felt my nostrils flare wide on my sharp inhale.

But the increase in air didn't help my temper.

"You are being an asshole," I gritted out, hopping off the counter and crossing my arms. "And stop growling at me. I'm a grown woman, not an idiot. Otherwise"—I poked him in the chest—"next time I won't want to confide in you."

He caught my hand, eyes still narrowed, temper still in the air.

Then, all of a sudden, it faded.

"I *am* being an asshole," he said. "I'm sorry."

I blinked at him, not wanting to let *my* temper go. "I didn't *not* tell you on purpose."

His mouth hitched up, sending my pulse spiking, a tendril of heat between my legs. "I know, tigress." A breath. "I fucking hate the idea of that bastard somehow still having the ability to touch your life."

I paused.

Because I hated that too.

But...I was still annoyed.

He leaned down, took my mouth in a kiss that both surprised me and stole the air from my lungs. "I like this new tough, take-no-shit Frankie." A beat before he pulled back, his smile huge. "So long as I get my sweet, but naughty Frankie in bed."

I blinked at him again.

Had to physically shake myself out of the stupor.

Something that was only accomplished because he turned back to the stove and finished dishing up dinner.

I stared at his back, at the protective man with the temper that had flared on my behalf, a temper he'd put away a heartbeat later when I'd called him on his shit.

I thought about what he'd just said, how he clearly wasn't upset about that fact.

And...my lips turned up.

Dreams into reality indeed.

I shook my head, happiness blooming in my middle.

"No guarantees," I said lightly.

Though, we both knew I was lying.

TWENTY-FIVE

LEX

Every inhalation brought the scent of disinfectant.

I'd been in enough hospitals that I wasn't uncomfortable, but it wasn't on my top ten places to visit, that was for damned sure.

Especially when I was waiting to be let back into a room, so Carter and I could interview a woman who'd been beaten and stabbed and shot, and then had nearly died.

And now was finally conscious and able to be questioned.

Whether or not she would actually be ready to talk about what had happened to her, or be *willing* to was another story.

"Lex."

I glanced up from the file I'd been reviewing and saw Attie striding through the waiting room. "I'll be right back," I told Carter, crossing to her.

"I was nearby," she said by way of explanation since I'd touched base with her about the letter earlier and made plans to drop it at her office. "Figured I would save you a trip."

"Right," I said, knowing that was both the truth and not the full story.

She gave without me pressing her. "Plus, I needed to see the face of Lex Blackwell, who's finally accepted his fate in life. And by fate"—she snagged the envelope I held out—"I mean, he —*you*—finally got your head out of your ass."

"Attie."

Her head whipped up, eyes narrowing.

"Open the fucking envelope," I muttered. "And focus on your own love life instead of mine."

"Kind of hard to do when you have no love life to speak of."

"Ats—" I began because I didn't like the note of sadness in that statement, but before I could really dig into that, she was tugging the paper from the envelope, eyes going to the paper.

"That wasn't an open invitation to feel bad for me," she said softly. "I'm not looking for love." A glance up at me, mouth quirked. "Mostly because it's way more fun to be single, and"—a shrug—"because I don't have the time or patience for men and their bullshit."

Well, that spoke of bitterness, didn't it?

Not that I was one to talk.

"Ats—"

She touched my hand, squeezed lightly. "I'm good," she said. "Hopelessly single and had my heart broken more than a few times, like every other woman on this planet. But I'm good." A beat. "Promise."

I studied her closely, focusing on the way she held my gaze, not hiding the past hurts in her eyes, but also not hiding from *me*, and I knew that this wasn't the right time or place for this conversation.

Knew I needed to let this go.

For the moment.

"What do you think of that?" I asked, nodding at the letter.

She exhaled, relief creeping into her eyes. Then she was all back to business. "I think that Francis Lyon is threatening his daughter—however obliquely, because he's not dumb enough to actually put it on paper." She folded the letter, tucked it back into the envelope. "But that it's definitely a threat and that means she—and *you*—need to be careful."

I nodded. "Unfortunately, I'm in agreement."

"I'll put this in the file," she muttered. "See if I can track down any chatter that might mean the threats are turning into action." She slid the envelope into the pocket of her blazer, looked back up at me. "Is she going to do it?"

"Move back to her father's house to put his *'affairs in order'?*" I scowled. "Fuck no, she's not going within a mile of that nightmare. It was hard enough for her to escape in the first place, and just because Francis Fucking Lyon has gotten it in his head to either reconcile with her or use her up like he uses up every other goddamned person, doesn't mean I'm letting her back into his sphere of focus."

Attie's brows lifted. "I don't disagree with you," she said, "but I'm also not sure that you get to make that call."

Unfortunately, she was right.

"Frankie doesn't want to be associated with him," I muttered. "She lived a nightmare—something you suspected—"

Attie nodded.

"She won't go back, not when she's fought so hard for the life she's built."

A long pause, but then Attie nodded. "Then I'll do everything in my power to help you prevent that."

A good woman. A good partner. An even better person. "Thanks, Ats."

Another nod, not acknowledging the gratitude, that sadness creeping back into her eyes. "I'll see you back at the office."

"Ats—"

She just tossed a wave my direction and turned on her heel, heading out of the waiting room. I didn't get a chance to stop her because Carter called my name, and I saw a nurse standing by his side.

No time to puzzle Attie out, to find a way to make the glimpse she'd just given me into those past hurts better.

I moved toward Carter, toward the nurse.

And I followed them back to a room that housed another woman whose life I wanted to make better.

She stared up at us with wide eyes, the bruise around her right one sporting a plethora of colors—deep purple to black to green to yellow. A scab on her top lip, narrow strips of bandages on her cheek, crisscrossing over dark blue sutures. A cast on one hand. A black plastic boot on a foot. Blankets tucked around her chest, hiding several knife wounds, a gunshot that had just missed hitting anything important by some fucking miracle, and the evidence of a beating.

"Will you tell us your name?" I asked softly, starting with a soft ball.

She didn't reply.

"What about why you were in the high school parking lot?"

Her lips pressed flat, but she didn't answer.

"Do you know who hurt you?"

Panic on her face, but those lips didn't release, didn't soften, her eyes didn't focus.

Wherever she was, it wasn't solely here in the present with us.

"Was it about Candy?"

She started at the name of the drug, eyes flashing with pain from the movement.

But she still didn't speak.

I gentled my voice. "We really need your help to get these people off the streets."

Nothing.

"Please," Carter interjected carefully. "We won't be able to help you unless you help us."

She turned her head to the side, gaze going to the wall.

He waited.

I waited, wondered how in the fuck I could push for some real answers without making things worse, without causing her to shut down further. Because there was a thick ass brick wall up between us and whatever thoughts were locked up in the woman's mind.

And...I didn't find a solution. Didn't have a brilliant idea to bust through that wall or unlock those thoughts.

And...the woman still didn't speak.

No matter what I said or how Carter probed or what levers we tried to push—hard and soft, gentle pushing and round about questioning, direct inquiries.

We only got silence in return.

Twenty-Six

I paused at the bottom of the stairs to Lex's apartment and wondered if I was doing the right thing.

But...the light was on inside.

And *my* light was on.

And...he hadn't come over.

And...

I was a new Frankie. I wasn't waiting on the sidelines, waiting for something to happen to me. I wasn't going to stand by and be too scared or nervous to assert myself. Not any longer. I could run a successful business, could manage twenty-four Cub Scouts during a cooking class. I wasn't a doll to be molded and posed and sat on a shelf.

So, I'd grabbed a tote bag, filled it with food and marched down my stairs, across Darlington's Main Street, and paused at the bottom of the exterior staircase to Lex's place.

Which suddenly seemed like it consisted of a thousand steps.

Could I make it up them?

Should I?

"Dammit," I muttered. "Yes, Frankie, you can, you should, and you're going to." Nodding to myself, hitching my tote up higher on my shoulder, I started climbing.

It *did* feel like a thousand steps.

A million.

But eventually I made it to the door.

And despite the short battle with myself, I managed to not delay—too long—before I lifted my hand and knocked on the door.

I didn't even doorbell ditch.

Probably because I would have killed myself tripping down the stairs if I'd tried.

Then the door swung open and everything suddenly came together, everything suddenly made sense.

This was where I was supposed to be.

Not the location.

But with this man.

But even as I was sitting in that, I was noticing that something wasn't right with him. No just *not right*, but that something was really, *really* wrong.

And I don't know what came over me.

Anger. Annoyance. A dash of hurt.

Something was wrong and he was *over here?*

Something was wrong and he wasn't with me?

Something was wrong and he didn't trust me to help?

I suddenly got why he'd been upset about the letter, but even as that clarity dawned, annoyance took over.

"Why are you here?" I asked, plunking my hands onto my hips, tote sliding down to my wrist and swinging wildly.

He blinked. "What?"

"Why are you"—I waved a hand between us—"*here?*"

He frowned, beautiful blue eyes clouded with confusion. "It's my apartment."

"Yeah," I said, shoving my way past him and moving into the

space, seeing it was as sparse and unlived in as the last time I'd been inside.

Which wasn't really a surprise since that wasn't all that long ago and he'd been spending most of his time in my apartment, but...it was something else that made me mad all the same.

He was a liar.

A big fat liar.

Because he was living his life as half-full as I was.

And that *pissed me off.*

"What are you doing?" I snapped, dropping my tote on the counter and crossing my arms.

He turned slowly from the door, brows furrowed. Then I watched his big chest expand and contract before he slammed it shut, flicked the lock.

And prowled toward me.

"Are you seriously coming in here like this?" he asked dangerously.

I'd be lying if I said my courage stayed firmly in place. Because it wavered as he came to me, all big and strong and now pissed-off male.

But I was New Frankie.

I held on to my courage, even if it shook and wobbled.

I lifted my chin. "I was over in my apartment, saw the lights on in yours, knowing you could see the lights on in mine." He stopped in front of me, the toes of his sock-clad feet brushing my shoes. He was big and brooding and intimidating, but...he wouldn't hurt me. I knew that in my belly, my heart, my soul. So, I went on. "I was waiting for you, and when you didn't come or call or reply to my text"—I shot him an arch look that I expected to piss him off but, incongruously, seemed to make his expression soften—"I decided to come over and see what the heck was wrong with you."

His mouth tipped up. "Yeah?" he asked silkily. "To see what was wrong with me?"

I narrowed my eyes. "You didn't reply," I said and waved a hand toward the kitchen. "And you clearly haven't eaten dinner."

"I could have stopped on the way home and gotten something."

He hadn't.

"You didn't," I said. "Because you wouldn't leave me to eat on my own."

His eyes warmed. "I wouldn't?"

"No." I felt that in my heart too. "So, I know something's wrong. I can see it in your face, honey." I reached up, cupped his jaw. "Tell me how I can make it better."

He stilled, expression clearing, going completely blank.

A pit opened up in my stomach. Fuck. Had I pushed this too far? Had—

"*Ack!*"

I squealed as he scooped me up and walked us fully into the kitchen, setting me onto the counter next to the sink. He nudged my legs apart, stood between them, our faces mere millimeters apart. "I had a shit day at work."

My heart was pounding—and not just because he was so close, not just because he'd shown me exactly how strong he was, sweeping me up and carrying me here, but because he'd given. He'd opened up.

"How can I make it better?" I asked quietly.

His mouth quirked. "By calling me on my shit and not letting me brood all night, tigress."

I ran my fingers through his beard, heart still pounding but my belly going soft.

Because I really liked this man.

"I can do that," I said. "But I can do more than that." I turned, reached for my tote bag, hauled it to me. "I'll fill your belly, let you watch something on TV that isn't a reality show, and then, later, we can talk about it."

He covered my hand with his own. "How about I cook for you, we watch something we *both* like, and after I give you a couple of orgasms, you return the favor, and then sleep in my bed all night?"

I shivered…because orgasms.

But also, "Is this your nice way of telling me that you can't talk about your case?"

Gentle in his face.

He leaned in, brushed his lips over my forehead. "Yeah, tigress," he murmured. "It's me saying I can't tell you what I'm working on." A beat. "Aside from the fact that I need a witness to talk to us, and I don't think she's going to."

My heart squeezed. "Is she scared?"

A nod. "Scared and traumatized and recovering from a lot of injuries."

I closed my eyes. "Damn," I whispered. "I'm sorry."

"I know you are, tigress."

I opened my eyes, knew it was time for me to lighten things up, knew that he'd given me the perfect opportunity with that nickname. "Tigress?"

He grinned. "With the way you keep calling me on my shit, the way you stormed in here," he teased, thankfully picking up on the light. "You're as fierce as a tigress." A beat. "Actually, I think you broke my toe when you stomped on it."

"I did not!" I exclaimed. "I distinctly remember *not* stomping on anything as I marched in here to put you in your place."

He gripped my hips, tugged me toward the edge of the counter. "I really think it might be broken."

I gasped, guilt threading through me. "No, it's not."

"Yes, it is."

Remorse rippled and grew, and it took a second, but eventually I picked up on it—on the teasing light in his eyes.

"I *think* you might be talking out of your ass," I grumbled.

"*This* ass maybe," he whispered, sliding a hand down, cupping mine.

I glared.

But it was fake.

Because inside I was happy.

Well and truly happy.

Twenty-Seven

Lex

Unfortunately, despite my promise of giving her several orgasms, Frankie fell asleep in my arms about halfway through the episode of the crappy cop show we'd negotiated to watch.

I didn't move, content to have her there.

Happy to hold her.

Knowing exactly how much it had cost her to stride that sexy ass of hers into my apartment and put me in my place.

Communicating exactly what she wanted from our relationship.

Because, yeah, it was a relationship, a real one, and one that was as important to her as it was to me—if her handing me my ass was any indication.

So, I felt like preening, like showing off.

She wasn't avoiding me or us, and she...

Was generous.

She cared.

She saw even what I'd had absolutely no intention of

sharing.

And she'd been fine knowing I couldn't tell her everything, so long as I'd given her something—and frankly, I'd given her more than I'd *ever* given Hailey.

Because she was...Frankie.

And the more time I spent with her, the more I understood that she was mine.

So, I waited for the episode to finish.

But I still didn't move, just held her through another show that I didn't pay any attention to because Frankie was in my arms and it wasn't anywhere near as interesting as the way her lashes fanned out over the tops of her cheeks, the pattern of freckles on her nose, how she'd relaxed into my arms, how she'd settled in my hold, how she trusted me enough to fall asleep in my arms.

"...reports of a new drug inundating local teen parties has brought community concern."

My gaze shot to the TV, locking onto the community news broadcast.

"Apparently called Candy, this drug looks like a manufactured sweet, but it is incredibly dangerous, carrying lethal amounts of fentanyl. It's been spotted at a handful of local parties, including one where several local teens were found unconscious. Roberta Franklin has more information," she said, tossing it to an on-scene reporter who was standing in front of several police cars, their light bars flashing red and white.

The reporter started breaking down the latest information she had—which was, thankfully, not everything, but it was enough that when my phone rang, I wasn't surprised it was Carter.

"Hey," I muttered after I managed to extract it and myself without waking Frankie.

"You see the report?"

"Yup." I said as I moved into the other room, toward the

window where I'd spent many an hour watching my woman live her life without me.

Carter sighed. "A fucking mess."

"Do you know who leaked it?" We were trying to keep shit quiet until we knew more—like if this was something that Lyon had his fingers in, or if the murders were related to another group. IDing the other man, along with the woman we'd found —or getting her to give us something—would also be helpful.

"Someone from the police department is all I can tell," Carter said. "Roberta has a high schooler and rumors are flying as they do in Darlington, so it's not a surprise that she sniffed this out."

"Damn. I—" But I didn't finish my thought because I could have sworn I saw something move outside the window, a shadow shifting in the distance, near the trees that lined the strip of land behind Frankie's shop and apartment.

"I know," Carter said with a sigh. "Not the attention we wanted. At least not until we know more. People are going to want answers and we don't have them."

News traveled fast in Darlington.

And this kind of news was going to send the community into a tizzy.

This wasn't voting on funding new jerseys for the local high school basketball team, or whether to close downtown for a holiday parade.

We were talking about dangerous drugs, and potentially the involvement of at least one seriously dangerous individual.

"Shit," I muttered as I focused that tree line, wishing I had my binoculars. But I'd brought them back to work, not needing them since I'd pretty much spent every free waking moment with Frankie. After a moment of not seeing anything—no shadows moving, no flickers of light, nothing glinting off metal or shining off skin, I decided that it had just been a product of the wind and me moving toward the window. A trick of the eye.

"I know," Carter said again.

I turned away, shifting my attention fully back to the conversation at hand. "You need to go into lockdown. Don't share any information with anyone except you and Chance. See if Cam can get anything else from the high school hockey coach. We pool our resources, plug any leaks, and if there's any connection to deeper shit"—like, say one Francis Lyon—"then we pass it off to Attie and the team for their investigation."

"I don't like this," Carter muttered.

"Did you search the database for our Jane Doe?"

"I've searched every database I have access to, and the ones you passed along as well." A sigh. "There are hundreds of missing persons that match her description, and I'm working through them one by one. But so far, I don't have any hits that match up with who we have."

Which spoke to someone like Francis Lyon being involved.

She was too fucking scared to speak, and if she was being trafficked, it was likely that she had few connections, fewer resources, and might not ever find the courage to tell us what had happened to her and why.

Carter's tone was filled with frustration. "We need to make sure the hospital doesn't discharge her until we know it's safe."

I felt that too. Deeply. "The doctors say it'll at be another week before she's cleared for that, but I have the social worker on it. They confirmed we'll get a plan in place before she's out. But you know as well as I do, we can't keep her there if she wants to go. There's no evidence that she was involved in the homicides"—no footage or physical corroboration that we'd found to date—"so it's not like we'll have anything legal to keep her in town either."

"Fuck, man, this is a mess," Carter growled. "The community is going to be up in arms with these news reports. We've got two dead guys, a bunch of kids who've been overdosing, and drugs circling but no idea who's actually dealing."

In other words, we had shit-all.

"We just have to be calm and focused and work this by the book," I said. "Lock it down so we're the only ones with all the information, be patient while we put the pieces together, and know that we'll get to the bottom of it all."

"We fucking better," Carter grumbled. "Because I don't want this shit in my town."

"We'll get Darlington back to puking up romantic Christmas movies with lumbersexual heroes and women who've left the big city to help out at their grandparents' bakery in no time."

Carter was silent.

But only for a moment.

Then he burst out laughing.

"Where the fuck do you come up with this shit?"

I came up with it because it was true...and also because I needed my friend—okay, my brother—to laugh.

To release the tension and the strain.

I knew he needed assurances, and while I didn't necessarily believe everything I'd said—because I'd been doing this long enough to understand that shit didn't always get solved just because I wanted it to—I was putting it out there.

Because Carter knew as well as I did that there was a chance this would all go bad.

Because he needed to hear it could work out differently.

Because I needed to say it.

Because a woman was in the hospital with gunshot and knife wounds who needed it to be true.

Because the woman who'd been sleeping soundly in my arms, trusting me to watch out for her needed her town to be safe.

And I was going to do every fucking thing in my power to make that happen.

Twenty-Eight

The bell rang above the door to Earthly Delights, and I glanced up.

Immediately, my heart rolled over in my chest, squeezed.

Because this was like all of those months ago—Lex prowling in through the front door, his big body taking up more than his fair share of space, but his presence stealing through the air, wrapping around me, drawing me in like a siren's call.

Only this time I wasn't tongue-tied as I helped him pick out the proper sleep supplement.

I was tongue-tied as he rounded the counter, paused with his boots an inch away from my ballet flats, his body warm and close and *there*, his scent in my nose, his heat on my skin, his hand cupping my cheek. "Hi, tigress," he murmured.

My inhale was sharp—mostly because my heart was pounding.

And because he was sexy as fuck.

"Hi," I murmured back. "What are you doing here?"

"Making sure you eat lunch." He bent, rubbed his nose against mine. "Because I've noticed that you tend not to." A chastising look.

"It's not because I'm not wanting to eat," I whispered. "I just get busy and my kids have school during the day. It's not easy for me to step away."

A kiss to the tip of my nose. "I know." He pulled back slightly, those blue eyes hitting mine. "So, when I have the time, I'm making sure you work on that gorgeous ass of yours."

"I hope that's code for pancakes from the diner," I muttered.

"I know what tea you drink, baby. Know that you prefer honey that's been made from wildflowers. I know you work long hours and you're so much more beautiful inside than you are on the outside—"

My lungs froze.

"And yes, it's code for pancakes at the diner. Plus"—he leaned back enough to pull something out of his pocket—"extra dark chocolate with sea salt for dessert."

Usually pancakes *were* my dessert.

But I would never turn down that brand of chocolate.

And I knew I'd never turn down time with this man.

So, I touched my mouth to his, grabbed my purse, keys, and phone...and walked to the door.

And then I flipped the sign to closed.

———

I was late.

Lunch hadn't been all that long—Lex did have a job and an active investigation to get back to—but it had put me a bit off my schedule.

And then add in that Mitzi, one of my best—and most challenging customers—had come in just after I'd reopened.

Which meant lunch had been followed by an hour of

helping her and jumping to the register to ring up purchases then back to her to break down the difference between a selection of vitamins and if she'd be better off with a powdered variety, a capsule, or a gummy.

I'd advised.

I'd rung up other customers.

My to-do list had grown.

And now I was late.

I *could* have skipped making the treat I was packing up, but I always liked to bring something when we went to dinner with all the Jacksons. And I meant *all* of them—the five brothers, including Cam, who was dropping in for the night after a nearby hockey game (he played for the Oakland Eagles and was thoroughly impressive), their adopted children—Lex and Sophie—the spouses who had married into the fold, the grandkids, and the strays—like me—that had been picked up along the way.

It always made for a loud and boisterous and fun evening, and though I knew that they would never expect me to bring anything, I always did anyway.

Probably, I should have stuck to granola. I could have whipped that out quickly and it would be tasty, and Martha—the Jackson matriarch—would have been thrilled.

Everyone loved it.

But...I'd wanted to up my game.

Because now I was dating one of theirs.

And this was...different and more important and—

I'd wanted to bring something...special.

So, I'd gone all out with a new protein bar recipe. It had whole oats and a narrow strip of freshly made lemon curd.

They were freaking delicious, if I did say so myself.

Probably why I'd needed to make a second pan. Because—cough—I might have sampled a little too much.

But they were healthy!

I slung my purse over my shoulder, grabbed my phone and

shoved it into my back pocket. Lights on—one inside, one outside. Jacket tucked under my arm. Lemon bars in hand.

"Right," I muttered. "Let's get a move on, Frankie."

Exhaling, shoring my spine, I move through the door, locked up, then hustled down the stairs and toward my car, bleeping the locks, tucking the lemon bars safely in the trunk. I slammed the lid shut, straightened, and...

Froze.

Nape prickling.

Hands clenching into fists.

Slowly, I swiveled my head, expecting to see...what?

Because there was nothing there, just shadows and silence.

Except—

A crunch had me jumping, whipping around, gaze torn from the tree line just in time to see a pair of headlights turning into the parking lot behind Earthly Delight.

I clamped a hand to my chest, heart pounding, my other hand clenched into a fist.

The car pulled to a stop.

The window whirred down, and everything inside me relaxed when I realized it was Lex, that it was Lex's car.

That Lex was here.

I inhaled, exhaled.

A creak. The car door opening.

And then Lex was there, his hand cupping my cheek. "What, baby?"

My teeth pressed into my bottom lip for a second, processing what I thought I'd seen, debating between telling him and knowing it was probably just my imagination. And then knowing, deep in my belly, that if I didn't tell him and it *wasn't* nothing—

He would be *pissed.*

"I saw something in the trees."

His response was immediate, his palm leaving my cheek, gaze

whipping around, moving so he was between me and that side of the parking lot. "Inside," he ordered, reaching for his gun. "Lock the door and call Carter and Chance. Tell them to get their asses down here."

"But—"

"Inside, tigress," he said more firmly, gun drawn, free hand lifting to grip my arm, keeping me next to him as he walked us backward toward the exterior stairs. "No arguments now, yeah?" A little softer. "I need you safe, and I need Carter and Chance to come help me."

"I—" My throat was tight and I cleared it. Because he was right and I didn't want to delay him getting help. Not when it might be dangerous. "Okay," I whispered.

A nudge. "Now, baby."

I realized we'd reached the bottom of the stairs, so I turned, ran up them, unlocking my door as quickly as I could with shaking hands, with fumbling fingers. I pushed inside, glancing back and finding Lex's gaze rotating between my apartment and the bushes.

"Lock up." Because, of course, he'd notice I paused. "And call Carter, baby."

"Okay," I said. "B-be safe."

A nod and then I was closing the door, hitting the latch, pulling my phone from my purse.

And calling Carter.

All while knowing that the man I was falling for was walking into a dangerous situation.

That might implode and ruin everything we were building.

Twenty-Nine

LEX

I t was too much of a coincidence to *not* be something.

And I was an idiot for having ignored it during my conversation with Carter the other day.

Shadows moving in the tree line.

By Frankie's place.

I should have hauled Carter's ass over here the first time—

Crack!

I dove to the pavement, hearing the bullet whizz over my head.

"Fuck," I muttered, crawling toward my car, bracing for the next shot to be fired, for the next bullet to fly. I braced for the white-hot pain that would come, shooting down my torso, my arms and legs, pinning my body to the ground.

But it didn't.

Not as I got my ass behind my car, got my phone out and called for backup.

Not as my eyes adjusted, night vision coming into focus, and I decided moving toward the trees was better than standing with my ass flapping in the wind while waiting for backup or for more bullets to come.

I didn't have a vest, didn't have anything more than my service weapon.

I didn't love that I was charging into a potentially deadly situation without backup.

But I knew that if I wanted a chance at getting the asshole who'd fired at me, who'd been lurking in the bushes waiting for the woman I'd fallen in love with, then I needed to act now.

I moved quietly to the trunk of the car, rounded it silently, gaze swiveling, searching for any signs of movement, any glint of metal, any noise that might speak to where that fucker might have gone, might still be holed up and—

Move.

I ran, crouched down, a small target, hauling ass over to the dumpster and pausing behind that cover.

Still searching, only doing it more thoroughly because I was closer, could see further into the shadows.

Nothing.

A breath. Seeking my next cover.

Then moving toward the trees, pausing behind a thick trunk, listening, eyes searching—

Bug noises starting up again.

The hoot of an owl.

That was when I relaxed slightly.

Whoever had been here had gone.

Still, I was cautious as I slipped out from behind the tree, my gun drawn, moving quietly through the grove of trees—

Almost missing it.

The shell casing glinting in the moonlight.

Careless? Or a message?

I moved deliberately through the copse of trees, searching, ensuring that they were indeed empty before I went back to that shell casing and pulled out my phone, taking a picture of it, and when the flash came, seeing something else.

A piece of paper with some sort of flower on the back.

A boot print.

Indents were someone had knelt.

I didn't have any gloves, so I snapped more pictures, tried to capture everything I could while I waited for the cavalry to show up.

I pulled a pen from my pocket, lifted one corner of the paper—

There weren't a lot of words on that scrap of paper. I took a picture of the writing without really processing it, same as the symbol on the back. Then lifted my phone, glanced at the screen, zoomed in and—

Fuck.

Because there weren't a lot of words that *were* there...

But what they said had me tearing from the trees, sprinting across the parking lot, taking the stairs up to Frankie's apartment two at a time.

Because the note had read:

Francesa Lyon
126 Main Street
Darlington

I pounded on the door just as two Darlington PD squad cars squealed up to Earthly Delights—one stopping in the front, the other blocking off the parking lot to the back. Another SUV was right behind them, and skidded to a stop at the entrance of the alleyway.

"Hello?" came the voice from inside.

Frankie's voice.

My relief nearly sent me to my knees.

"Open the door, baby."

I needed to see her. I needed to make sure her apartment was secure. Then I needed to meet Carter and Chance downstairs and let them know what the fuck was happening.

I made eye contact with Carter when he hopped out of the SUV just as I heard the lock click open, and lifted a finger.

He nodded.

Frankie cracked the door, her eyes wide, her skin pale. "Are you okay?"

I decided not to mention the gunshot.

That could come later.

"Fine," I told her, squeezing her shoulder as I nudged her back, closed and locked the door. "Stay right here, okay?"

"I—" She pressed her lips together, released them. Nodded. "Okay."

I made short work of walking through the space, was aided by the fact that it was small and there weren't that many walls or rooms to clear. Then I was heading back for the front door, reaching for the handle.

"Are you—"

I turned back, feeling pressured and in a fucking hurry, knowing I needed to get outside to the guys, but one look at her face told me that Frankie needed me more. I pulled her close, wrapped my arms around her. "I'm good. You're good, baby." A kiss to the top of her head. "I need to get down there and meet the guys. You stay here, and I'll fill you in as soon as I can, yeah?"

She leaned back, stared deep into my eyes. Then she nodded, stepped back. "Be safe."

My heart squeezed.

Then I was through the door, not even having to stop and call to her to lock it before I heard the bolt engage. Smiling somehow—because my woman was fucking smart and beautiful and had a steel-lined spine—I pounded down the stairs. Carter saw me coming, breaking away from the group he'd been speaking to. Attie, I realized, and a couple of uniforms from the Darlington PD.

Attie trailed him as he walked toward me, her gaze sweeping me up and down. "Considering you're not bleeding," she said lightly, "I'm guessing the gunshots missed."

"Gunshot," I corrected softly because it was clear that she was worried, even if she was trying to keep everything playful. "And it missed. I cleared the trees but we need to set up a barrier, and we need lights and…" I took a breath, tried to keep my head level, my anger under wraps as I tugged my phone from my pocket, opened the photo app. "And I need to show you what I found."

Because it was a mindfuck.

Because it spoke to exactly who was involved.

Because it held the proof of a connection I'd really been hoping wasn't there.

And that link, the piece that held it all together…

Was Frankie.

THIRTY

FRANKIE

I'd waited a long time for the knock to come at my door the second time, nerves eating at me, tearing up my insides, causing my hands to tremble, and my muscles to tense so fiercely I knew I was going to be sore tomorrow.

It was different from the abject terror I'd felt that first round, knowing that Lex was out there alone, fighting those monsters in the shadows.

Protecting me and risking himself.

With Carter and Chance on their way but Lex still very much alone.

I'd felt that deep after I'd hung up my phone, knowing that help was coming, unsure if it was going to be enough, if it was going to be here soon enough.

Knowing that this wasn't about the case Lex was working on with Carter and Chance.

That this had to be about me.

My father.

The lawyer who'd hadn't approached me again. I'd thought

Lex put an end to it with the confrontation, but I should have known.

If my father wanted something from me, he didn't just *stop.*

It was only when I was used up, useless, too much trouble that he backed off.

And his lawyer showing up should have clued me in. He'd decided I served a purpose again and he was going to get what he wanted.

And...because of that Lex and everyone down here was at risk.

I'd been on the wrong side of his cruelty. I knew exactly how he treated the people who were disposable to him.

And I knew more.

About the drugs. The women. The—

The knock about made me jump out of my skin.

I picked up my phone, pulled up the camera app as I strode toward it, waiting for it to load even as I called out, "Who is it?"

"Me, baby."

A second before the camera loaded, giving me a glimpse of him healthy and whole.

I flicked open the lock, pulled the door in, and threw my arms around his middle. "Oh my God," I whispered, squeezing him tight. "You're okay?"

Fingers sliding through my hair, drifting around my jaw, cupping it, and bringing my head up, my eyes to his. "I'm fine. Promise," he murmured, moving into me, shuffling me back into the apartment.

I found out why a second later.

Because he turned me, tucked me into his side, and I watched as Carter, Chance, and Agent Phillips moved into my apartment.

The expressions on their faces told me enough.

"What is it?" I whispered.

Agent Phillips held up a plastic bag with a piece of paper

inside. I frowned, moved from the circle of Lex's arms, drifting closer so I could see it, so I could read it.

"Why's my name on it?" I asked, heart pounding in the back of my throat, nerves starting right back up again.

"We were kind of hoping that you might give us some insight into that," Agent Phillips said, and I didn't miss that her voice was gentle, but that her eyes were sharp, taking in every fraction of my reaction. She started to drop the bag back to her side.

Which was the moment I was certain I gave her something else to take in.

Because I lurched forward, grabbed her wrist, and lifted it, bringing the zip top bag back up to eye level.

"I've seen that logo before."

———

My shop was in shambles.

The only difference was that this time I was sitting in the kitchen, watching it happen...

And my wrists weren't cuffed.

A bevy of agents and police officers were tearing through my stock room—though, in fairness, it was less tearing and more pulling out every box and bin and bag from every shelf and cabinet and closet.

At least I wasn't stuck supervising the dumpster cleanout—considering that it had been a few days since I'd tossed that initial box, I wasn't envious of whoever was spending their time digging around in the trash, in the rotten food and boxes of garbage.

Instead, I was digging my fork into the pan of lemon bars Agent Phillips—Attie to Lex, Ats to all who didn't want the agent to send a laser-like glare their direction—had retrieved for me, giving me something to do, to *eat* as I watched them go through boxes—opening, sorting, stacking, and occasionally bringing something to me to confirm what it was.

I wasn't practicing moderation in any way, shape, or form.

I'd already demolished half of the pan of lemon bars.

Because I was trying to distract myself from the fact that my shop looked like a bomb had gone off. Again.

But that wasn't all bad.

Okay, well, it wasn't great.

It was a nightmare, but also...there was a stack of boxes in the corner of the kitchen.

Which told me enough about the state of Lex's mind.

My telling them I'd seen the logo, had received shipments with it printed on the outside of several boxes a handful of times in my shop hadn't turned him cold. Neither had my explanation of the phone call and my effort to try and return them. Neither had my cooperating with the orders to trash them *instead* of shipping them back—and not having my concerned piqued.

He'd listened.

They'd *all* listened.

And their handcuffs had stayed in their holsters.

So, I could deal with my shop being in a bit of disarray (cue hysterical laughter).

I would put it back together again.

"Frankie."

The sharp tone of my name had my gaze jerking up from the half-decimated pan of lemon bars.

Lex was standing in the doorway, expression thunderous.

My gut clenched, worry pooling in my belly, but I didn't get to ask what the problem was because then he was storming across the room, gripping my wrist, pulling me up off the chair.

"What—"

I didn't even get to finish asking the question before he was dragging me from the room, up the interior staircase, and into my apartment.

He slammed the door, whipped around, eyes narrowed as though he were searching the apartment for any straggling police officers or FBI agents.

Luckily—or maybe not—it was empty.

"What the fuck are you doing?" he snapped.

Since that was my line, it took me a second to process it and then to formulate a response, and by then the storm that was Lex Blackwell had reached category one.

"You're sitting at that table, looking like someone punched you, when you probably gave us, gave Attie and the team the break we've been looking for all along."

I exhaled, some of the worry and hurt in me fading. "First of all—"

"And it's not your fault. How could you know that the boxes were connected with your father?"

Now, my heart squeezed.

Because I got it.

Because he thought that I was hurt and worried he might think—

"And you shouldn't be upset about the boxes and not mentioning them. You should be worried about why there was a fucking note in the trees with your goddamned name on it."

Well, no surprise, now I was *extra* worried about it.

"And I know you, Frankie," he snapped. "I know you and I love you and I'm not going to make the same idiotic mistakes again. I won't treat you like crap again. I won't distrust you. I know the person you are inside, and you're not like your father, baby."

My heart squeezed. But it was time to unleash the tigress. "Shut up."

His mouth closed, teeth clicking together.

"Good." I exhaled. "I apologize for that. It's rude to tell someone to shut up, but I just need you to stop talking for a few minutes."

A glimmer of something—amusement? frustration?—in his blue eyes, but he didn't talk, just dropped his hand to my waist, tugged me so I was pressed to him again.

"First of all," I said. "I'm sure you guys would have made the connection between the company and my father. You had the note and you are all very good at your jobs. And," I added a little more loudly when he opened his mouth, as though he were going to argue. "And," I said again, "I wasn't sitting there upset and worried about what you all were thinking about, or if you were thinking I was some sort of evil criminal. I was thinking about my store being a mess." I narrowed my eyes when I watched the protest form on his face. "And I know you'll help clean up—that's not the issue."

"Then what is?" he bit out.

"I'm trying to get to it," I bit back.

A glare.

I glared back.

"I was thinking that I was fucking lucky to have you!" I growled. "Thinking that I was lucky I knew you'd believed me, lucky that Agent Phillips and Carter and Chance did too. I was thinking that I was lucky because Attie had gotten me my lemon bars and they were delicious. And now I'm pissed off at you," I snapped. "Because you just yelled, *I love you* at me, and at the very least, that should have been accompanied by flowers or an orgasm because I fucking love you too, you big, stubborn oaf!"

I was on such a roll, that I didn't recognize his face had changed—from angry to soft to a dash of wicked. Not until he stepped close, pinning me between his body and the door.

"My tigress," he murmured, dropping his hands beside my head, boxing me in.

My heart skipped a beat, but I lifted my chin. "I'm mad at you."

"Fucking perfect and beautiful and *mine*." he said, cupping the side of my neck with his free hand. "I love you."

And...that mad disappeared.

I covered his hand with my own. "I love you too."

I loved saying the words.

I loved hearing them.

But most of all I loved watching what his face did when I spoke them to him.

"Fuck, baby," he whispered before his mouth dropped to mine, lips parting, tongue slipping in...

And then, for a long, long time, words were the last thing on my mind.

But they were sealed deep inside my heart.

And the next day, when I woke up, after an orgasm that had left me seeing stars, after he'd gone to work and I went downstairs and found Earthly Delights clean—as I'd somehow known it would be—I walked to the cash register, seeing the little basket of hemp bows...

Sitting beside a vase filled with the most gorgeous flowers I'd ever seen.

And I smiled.

Thirty-One

I strode into the office, hating that I'd left Frankie alone, glad I'd woken up early enough to make sure that her store was clean and ready for her to open in a few hours.

Glad I'd been able to catch the local florist as she opened up her shop, so I could pay an exorbitant amount for a vase of flowers that was currently sitting next to the register in Earthly Delights.

Because Frankie had been right.

I'd bellowed my feelings at her.

And...she'd turned full tigress.

And...she'd yelled at me.

And...she'd said those words back.

Fucking beautiful—the words, the way they settled over me, her face when I said them to her.

And that was why she deserved orgasms—something I'd accomplished last night to such an extent that she'd passed out and I'd gone back down to help the team wrap up the search, to start the cleanup I'd finished this morning—*and* flowers.

So...she'd get fucking flowers.

And orgasms.

And—

A punch to my stomach that was hard enough to shoot the air from my lungs. "Jesus, Attie," I huffed, rubbing the spot, and turning to glare at my friend and fellow agent. "What the fuck are you doing?"

"That's"—a nod toward my stomach—"for almost getting shot last night."

"I told you the bullet missed," I muttered, moving past her. "I was fine."

"I *saw* the bullet hole in the stucco, dumb fuck, I know *exactly* how close that shot was to taking your dumb ass out."

She was worried, so I tried to draw her out of that. "I prefer it when you refer to me as big *and* dumb," I quipped, bumping her shoulder with mine.

Half her mouth turned up. "Okay, so I know exactly how close that shot was to taking your big *and* dumb ass out."

"I know you do," I said moving forward—and because I was dumb *and* big, she had to move too, so she wasn't crushed.

Perks of being a big oaf.

Which had me thinking of Frankie again.

Which had me dodging another punch Attie tried to throw my way.

"Nice try," I told her, nudging her back, grinning when she stumbled. "Dumb *and* big, remember?"

She grinned. "I can't help it." A beat. "You look too fucking happy." Then she sobered. "I'm kidding. I'm glad for you. Truly." She squeezed my forearm. "And I'll be nice."

My brows lifted—maybe in question, maybe because nice wasn't really in Attie's personality. "Seriously?"

"Ugh," she muttered. "You're the worst partner ever."

"So you've said a time or a hundred," I teased.

Her expression turned just the slightest bit wicked. "Okay," she said. "How about this? *Truly*, I'm glad you finally got your head out of your ass."

That was more like the Attie I knew.

"In fairness, it's been out for a while."

A tilt of her head, her curls bouncing. "A whole week?"

"Maybe two," I quipped back.

She snorted.

"Now," I muttered. "Are you done giving me a hard time?"

"Depends," she said as we neared my office, slowing outside the closed door.

"On what?"

"You." A beat. "And if your head-removal abilities extend to getting your ass back on the case."

"You think the boss lady will let me be back on?"

"Yes," she said, her mouth was curving. "Especially if you stop playing the honorable hero who doesn't want to risk the case and start playing the kickass agent who has the highest close rate in our department. Can you do that?"

"That honorable agent," I said, because I couldn't bring myself to use the word *hero*, "got shot at and found his woman's name on a fucking piece of paper connecting her to an open case. He's activated straight to kickass and take no prisoners."

Attie nodded. "Good." A beat. "Because we need you."

I reached for the door handle.

"Although..."

Christ.

"What, Attie?"

Her deep brown eyes sparkled with humor. "Are you more mad about the piece of paper or the bullet?"

I pushed open the door, turned back. "I'm talking to the boss and then you're debriefing me on where we're at."

"Lex?"

Jesus Fucking Christ.

"Yeah, Ats?"

She smiled and it was genuine this time. "I'm glad you're back."

———

It was late.

I'd been working a shit ton of hours over the last week—certainly more than I'd slept, with far fewer breaks than I normally took, and with far less time with Frankie than I wanted.

But I was finally caught up with what I'd missed, Attie, the guys, and I all had a plan with the new information, and—

It was confirmed.

The box we'd pulled from the dumpster, the one with the supplements Frankie had thrown away...

It was a powdered form of Candy.

Francis Lyon was peddling drugs in Darlington.

And he was using his daughter's shop to make that happen.

The question was...how long had it been happening? And also, I supposed, what in the fuck Lyon was going to do now that we'd figured out what he was doing?

Move on to a new dealer?

Punish his daughter?

Find another location to peddle from?

I parked, got out of my car, gaze swiveling as I crossed the street and moved up the exterior stairs to Frankie's apartment. Her lights were off, but after she'd stormed over to my place the week before, I sure as shit wasn't going to risk her getting out of bed, leaving the warm safety of her home, all just to put me in my place.

Plus, I'd left her sleeping this morning.

I wanted to eat, crawl into bed, and fall asleep with the scent of her in my nose.

I reached for the knob—

The door swung open.

Frankie was standing there in a short robe hitched around her middle, feet bare.

Legs bare, the hem of that robe teasing the tops of her thighs.

"I saw you on the camera," she whispered. "The one you put at the bottom of the stairs."

Because I was working a lot.

Because she was alone.

Because I'd had Carter and Chance help me wire up her entire place.

"You should have stayed in bed, baby," I told her.

"I was waiting for you." Her fingers went to the tie of her robe, tapping the knot, drawing my focus back to that clinging black fabric...and what was beneath it. "You hungry, honey? I made—"

"What do you have on, tigress?" I asked instead of answering, moving forward and hitching an arm around her waist, taking us both inside.

"Just a robe," she said, a little breathless.

My cock twitched. "And underneath it?"

Her lips parted on a shaky exhale, but her eyes flared with heat. "Why don't you find out?"

A quick movement and the door was closed.

Another and the lock was engaged.

One more and she was up in my arms and I was walking her toward the bed.

I was hungry.

I was going to eat.

But it sure as fuck wasn't going to be food.

I dropped her to the mattress, reached for the knot.

For the record, she had nothing on beneath that robe.

And it was fucking glorious.

THIRTY-TWO

FRANKIE

"You look happy."

I turned away from the sight of Caleb, one of the Jackson brother's and Kim's husband, running along the waves, Cole—his son—at his heels doing his best to take him down.

The sun was just beginning its downward trek, not quite sunset, but the beginnings of orange and pink were streaking across the sky.

Pretty.

The perfect temperature.

Even the wind had calmed, so I wasn't spending the entire time spitting out my hair because the breeze was blowing it into my mouth.

I was just sitting on the sand, picking through the crumbs of my granola bars.

Crumbs because I'd been inspired by my lemon bars and so instead of dark chocolate and freeze-dried raspberry, I'd made a lemon curd, dried blueberry, and poppy seed protein bar.

They'd been a hit.

And I'd meticulously carb-counted so Caleb, Kim, and their type 1 diabetic son didn't have to. Anything to make their lives —and help them get some sleep occasionally—easier.

Not that you would know he had a disability.

They had it so down with his pump nowadays that the average passerby would think he was just a typical kiddo.

Unfortunately, he had far more responsibilities on his tiny shoulders.

And Kim's. And Caleb's.

So, I did anything I could to make their lives a little easier.

And now I got to sit next to my friend, enjoy the night air, and just be in this moment. It had been a month since the note found in the shadows, since my shop had been pulled apart and drugs had been found in the boxes I'd disposed of.

And in another that had arrived but I hadn't had a chance to open yet.

And both were connected to my father.

Who was still in custody.

Who had been charged with a half dozen felonies.

Whose case was still being investigated.

Who hadn't tried to contact me via his lawyer, nor any one phone call—not that I wanted that. Unless I could turn double agent and find out something that helped the case against him.

Then again, he probably knew I was dating the FBI agent who'd arrested him.

Considering everyone seemed to think he had eyes everywhere.

I didn't doubt that. I just...

It would be really nice if they could assure me that my father would never darken my door again. I didn't like looking over one shoulder. I much preferred my version of life that had been leaving him and my past behind and building a peaceful future in Darlington.

"Frankie?"

I turned away from the waves, rolled back the mental conversation in my mind, and realized that Kim was being nice.

Mostly because she was being Nosy Lite.

Wanting the details, but not digging around with a dull spoon for every single piece of information—like Misty or Maggie or even Raven would.

Probably because she'd been in our group for a shorter amount of time.

We hadn't corrupted her yet.

Grinning, I bumped my shoulder against hers. "I'm happy. Really happy and settled in a way I never thought was possible. Lex is..." I sighed. "He's everything I've ever hoped for. And"—I turned to her—"I really like the person I am with him. It's like... I'm *me*, you know?"

Kim's expression was beyond gentle. "Yeah, honey. I know *exactly* how that feels."

"Mom!"

Cole barreled in, little legs moving in a flurry as he collided with Kim and took her down to the sand.

"Got you!" he said and kissed her cheek.

And seriously, my ovaries just about exploded.

I needed one of those.

Badly.

With Lex's blue eyes.

Kim grinned as she wrapped her arms around him and maneuvered to her feet, blowing a raspberry into his neck. "Stinker," she said, shaking her head, sand falling in a shower around her.

"I'm fast, Mom!"

"You sure are," she agreed, putting him down when he wriggled.

"I'm hungry."

"Hi, Hungry."

I giggled.

The look he shot her—then me, because of my amusement at the joke—was far too old for his years, that was for damn sure.

I knew Kim felt it too.

Because I saw it written into the lines of her face.

"Well, I guess we should get you some dinner, huh?" she asked.

"Yup." He popped the p at the end. "I'll get Dad."

And then he was off and running again.

I helped Kim pack up their stuff, waved off her offers of joining them for dinner. "I'm full up on lemon curd and blueberries." I gave her a hug. "Plus, it's such a beautiful night that I want to sit and watch the sunset."

Kim squeezed me back. "Okay," she said, dropping her arms and picking up her backpack of supplies, the blanket she'd been sitting on. "But I owe you dinner soon."

"So long as you make your apple pie for dessert."

She laughed. "You know Caleb would never let me make anything else."

Cole came in for a hug and dash, sprinting off through the dunes. Caleb gave me a squeeze and said with a conspiratorial wink, "Apple pie imminent."

I grinned, waved, and settled back into the sand.

And I watched the oranges and reds and pinks creep across the sky. I watched the navy slowly slide into place behind them, drawing the world into night.

The moon came out.

Stars began to twinkle.

Waves crashed in a perpetual, peaceful rhythm.

It was only when the wind began to pick up again that I realized how late it had grown. How *dark* it was.

My stomach flipped, and I hurried through the motions of packing up.

I needed to go back to the apartment, to start dinner.

Lex had been working insane hours and he would be tired and hungry...hopefully for both food and me.

Grinning, I made my way up the path, paused to slip on my sandals at the end of boardwalk.

I stepped out from between the dunes.

And *that* was the moment when I realized how stupid I'd been.

THIRTY-THREE

LEX

My eyes were blurry and my head fucking pounded.

It was way later than I'd intended on working, the world outside my office windows dark.

But I'd found it.

The final piece in the long ass paper trail, shell company after shell company after fucking *shell company*.

I typed it into my computer, pulled the paper from the stack I'd been painstakingly going through and made a half dozen copies before I scanned it and added it to my file on my computer.

The exciting world of the FBI.

It wasn't all storming buildings and drawing my gun.

I also spent time—too much fucking time in my opinion—building cases and *not* taking down bad guys.

But that was the process, that was the job.

We had to have certain parameters in place so we could be sure those bad guys remained where we wanted them—behind bars and not on our streets.

And I wanted Francis Lyon behind bars permanently.

Away from his daughter.

Away from Darlington.

Away from all the fucking innocent people whose lives he constantly fucked up.

And I'd found the final piece that the U.S. attorneys we were working with on this case wanted.

The nail in the coffin for Francis Lyon.

Fucking *finally*.

I emailed the boss and the rest of the team, spent way too fucking long organizing the printed copies, and was just going to head down the hall to Attie's office when there was a knock on the door.

Perfect timing.

Ats was standing outside my office door.

I waved her in, grabbing the file as I stood up, as I moved toward her. "Fucking finally," I said. "I found it, Ats—"

"Why the fuck are you still here?" she snapped.

I rocked back on my heels, eyes going wide, irritation blooming in my belly. "Jesus, Attie. I just cracked the case—"

"Francis Lyon was released from custody four hours ago."

"*What?*"

Attie shook her head. "I just got word from the boss, who just got word from *her* boss, and—"

I shoved the papers at her and she fumbled with catching them, causing a confetti of eight and a half by elevens to scatter over my carpet. But I didn't give a fuck, not when I was striding to my desk, picking up my phone, jabbing at the screen.

The call to Frankie rang in my ear.

And rang.

And *rang*.

Her voicemail came on and I hung up. Immediately dialed again.

More ringing.

More voicemail.

"Jesus fucking Christ," I muttered, my stomach twisting itself into knots as I called one more time, as I got voicemail again. I shoved it in my pocket, grabbed my keys from my desk drawer. "I'm going to Frankie's." I scribbled onto a piece of paper, shoved it at Attie, nearly upending the papers a second time. "That's her number. You have her other information. Start a trace on it."

"Lex," she began.

"I *need* to go, Ats," I said, moving past her, striding for the door.

"I'll call when I get a ping on her location."

I nodded and kept moving.

Out the door.

Down the stairs because I didn't want to wait for the fucking elevator.

Out to the parking lot.

To my car.

There was a note slipped between one of my windshield wipers and the glass.

Fuck.

My stomach churned, part of me already knowing what was going to be inside it.

I snagged the paper, saw that fucking flower logo on the back, and wanted to tear it into a thousand pieces, to set it on fire, to burn it.

Instead, I unfolded it.

Back off.
Or she'll be the one to get hurt.

Then, heart pounding, I crumpled it into a ball, shoved it in my pocket, and unlocked my car.

I got in, drove like a fucking bat out of hell to Darlington, blowing up Frankie's phone the entire way.

She didn't pick up.

Attie called to say she hadn't gotten a ping for several hours, that her last known location was the beach in town.

Where she'd met up with Kim, Caleb, and Cole.

Maybe they were distracted and playing.

But when I called them, they said they'd left hours ago.

I turned onto Main Street, screeched up to the curb in front of Earthly Delights.

The shop was dark.

As was her apartment.

And fucking empty when I searched inside.

Maybe her phone had taken a dive into the ocean.

I pounded down the stairs, got back into my car, drove the couple of blocks to the beach.

Got out, engine running, door open, sprinting down the boardwalk, reaching the end of the wood and about to step onto the sand.

When I caught a glimpse of something nestled in the grains of silica and quartz and froze.

I bent, pulling out my phone, flicking on the flashlight...

Bile burned the back of my throat.

Because halfway covered with sand was a familiar glass container.

Familiar because it belonged to my woman.

Thirty-Four

Frankie

My head pounded even as I processed that I was laying on something very soft.

Peeling my eyes open slowly, I waited for the darkness to clear, for the pain to increase from the sudden influx of light—

Only it didn't.

The darkness or the pain.

Because where I was it was pitch freaking black.

Not a sliver of light anywhere that I could detect.

And that was...terrifying, stifling, *suffocating*.

"Breathe," I whispered, slowly testing out my limbs, bending my fingers, flexing my feet, finding that soft again, feeling a silky fabric beneath my fingertips, the cushiness beneath my toes.

Where was I?

I'd watched the sunset, been drawn into the colors streaking across the sky, the stars and the moon.

I'd found peace.

And then I'd found...blackness.

A flash of the man in the dark suit, the crisp white shirt, the silken black tie.

And the fear that had pooled in my belly overflowed to my limbs, filled my body.

I'd turned to run—

Then blackness.

I slid a hand out, feeling across the softness, searching the darkness, finding the edge of what I was laying on. A bed, most certainly, but it wasn't until I pushed up to sitting, dangled my feet over the edge, felt the soft brush of carpet beneath my bare toes that I knew for sure.

And another truth was growing in my belly.

The silky bedspread. The plush pillow that had been supporting my head. The luxurious carpet between my toes.

I turned in the darkness, hand still extended, and—

Felt my fingers brush against the wooden pole that rose from the corner of my childhood bed, which pointed up toward the ceiling and formed one corner of the canopy overhead.

I used to love how the fabric draped, the way the light filtered through it, how it made my room cozy and warm and *mine*.

Not much had been truly mine.

That bed had been.

I'd picked it out. *I'd* slept in it. I—

Was reminiscing when I should be figuring how the fuck to get out of here.

Using the edge of the bed as a marker, I began to carefully shuffle toward the door. Hands out, toes curled. Prepared to run into something, and hoping that I wouldn't break a toe.

But nothing had changed from what I remembered, and before long, I was at the door, fingers on the knob, wrapping around the cool metal, muscle in my arm flexing as I prepared to depress the lever—

"I wouldn't do that if I were you."

I froze.

Stilled.

I *should* have used that doorknob, should have gotten the hell out when I got the chance.

But the voice didn't belong.

The voice shouldn't be here.

A light flicked on, blinding me, even more so as I whirled around, the brightness inundating my senses, stealing the revelation...

For a moment.

Because it sent me blinking, my eyes watering...until I saw my father sitting in the corner of my childhood bedroom.

"Henry is outside that door," he said, pushing up from the armchair. "And he wouldn't take kindly to you wandering off on your own."

I reached behind me, nails digging into the wood.

I wanted to yank at the handle, to *run*—

But I didn't. I *couldn't*, God help me.

"Henry?" I asked softly.

"You met him at the beach."

Tall. Big. Not gentle. With the dark suit and the crisp shirt and the narrow tie.

And the scary, *scary* eyes.

More digging into the wood, my nails not finding any purchase, my fingers cramping from the effort.

"Why am I here?" I rasped.

A slight pause then, "Why should you be anywhere else?"

My mouth fell open. My fear cleared. Because...was he fucking insane?

"Why did you come to my shop before you were—" I clamped my lips together for a moment, cutting off the mention of being arrested. Because he was here and I didn't know if it was because he'd used his resources to get out legally—though, I'd like to think that would be something Lex would communicate to me, say, before some guy named Henry with scary eyes kidnapped me.

"I'd given you long enough for that little"—he waved a hand dismissively—"adventure of yours. It's time to come home."

Oh. Fuck. No.

"That's not happening."

His brows shot up, probably because I'd never denied him anything before.

"Why are you out of jail?"

A shrug. "I have good attorneys."

I snorted. "I bet." His brows shot up further, but I had more thoughts, knew I needed to be smart, needed to think, needed to figure out how to get the hell out of this nightmare and back to my life in Darlington.

I wished there was a panic button.

I wished I had my phone.

I wished I could call Lex and he would just magically appear, scoop me up, and carry me the hell out of here.

Which meant I needed to buy myself some time.

"Why did you think me coming home would be a good idea?" I said, pushing off the door—and away from the scary ass Henry supposedly on the other side of it.

"You're my daughter. You belong here."

"Your daughter you haven't spoken to for years." I shook my head, gaze scanning. There had been a landline at my vanity. Maybe it was still there?

I drifted that way.

"I always knew exactly where you were."

Well *that* was creepy.

"And you used my store—my livelihood that I scrapped and worked my butt off for to sell drugs, didn't you?"

He slowly rose from the chair. "What did you say?"

My heart started pounding a little more quickly and I continued toward the vanity, trying to glean a look at the gleaming wooden surface. This whole room was like a creepy ass shrine, so I hoped that it was still—

There.

Sitting on the edge of the wood was a phone.

The only question was could I get a call out before my father realized what I was doing and Scary Henry came back in.

All I knew was that I had to try.

"I said"—I searched for a distraction then decided just... what the hell...and kept with it, both the inching toward that phone *and* the going with it—"that you used my shop to peddle your drugs."

His expression clouded and he continued moving toward me.

And I continued moving toward that phone.

"They found them," I said, bumping into the edge of the wooden tabletop, one hand going back to steady me, to reach for that phone. "*I* put the pieces together"—I increased my volume, covering the sound of me lifting the receiver, breathing a bit easier when I heard the faint dial tone—"I saw the symbol. Realized it was from the shipments that I hadn't ordered"—fingers fumbling, I felt for the nine, for the one, for the one again—"and," I said, still talking loudly, now over the voice on the other edge—"I don't know why you knocked me out and why you brought me back to this crappy old mansion on Clearwater. I don't live here anymore, and I don't want to. I want to go home and I want help to do it."

"You're going to stay here," he said quietly.

I carefully hung up the phone, hoping to hell that he didn't see it, hadn't heard it. "I'm not going to stay. I'll never stay. You can try to keep me, but I'll just wait for my opportunity and go again."

His face changed.

It had already been scary, already been sending my pulse skipping through my veins.

Now, whatever warmth that had been on his face disappeared.

Like he'd been pushed to the edge with the arrest, the weeks in jail. Like he'd been pushed even closer with me not waking up and being immediately obedient.

Like he now had one foot hanging over that edge with my threats.

"You're going to stay here," he said quietly, but his tone was deadly and icy cold, sending a shiver down my spine. "Because if you don't, your FBI agent is going to pay the price."

My father had already tried to fuck up Lex's life once.

My father had already tried to control *mine* until I felt as though I couldn't think or speak or *breathe* on my own.

And so when he stepped close to me, face just millimeters from mine, threats in the air, frost in his eyes and added softly, but no less deadly, "And I will enjoy every second of watching the life, seeing his hopes, his dreams squeezed out of him."

There was a noise in the hall, something I couldn't place.

But I barely had time to focus on it.

Because *that* was when I snapped.

THIRTY-FIVE

LEX

The call came in when I was less than two minutes out from my next destination.

I'd barely had the wherewithal to get my shit together after finding that container at the beach.

Barely had made it back downtown to Chance and Carter's firm.

Barely had been able to call Attie.

True to form, though, she was on top of it when I was struggling.

She was still tracking Frankie's phone, and in the meantime, she'd put together a search grid, using Kim's departure time and local routes, calculating exactly how far Frankie could have been taken.

So, we'd started looking.

Carter and I starting with our section, my team split up and searching others. Chance and their dad on another.

But it had been too fucking long.

Too much bad shit could have happened.

My Frankie was with that man and—

Attie's voice came through the speakers. "She's at his mansion on Clearwater Lane."

That was what we were a mile out from. "How?" I rasped.

"She's okay," Attie said. "She got a call out, but his mansion is fucking loaded, Lex. You need to stop and wait for us to mobilize to get more people there before you and Carter go in—"

I slanted a glance toward the passenger's seat, saw Carter shake his head slightly.

Knew he was on the same page as I was.

Fuck, no.

We were *not* waiting.

I hit the button to end the call. Hit the button to reject it when it immediately rang again.

"Firepower?" I asked.

"Not much," Carter muttered, reaching for the bag at his feet, pulling out a rifle and snapping the pieces together as we bumped down the road. "Not enough, probably. You've got a plan?"

"Yeah," I said. "I'm driving this shit through the gates, through the front fucking door if I can manage it. "Then we're getting Frankie the hell out of here."

A beat.

Then Carter screwed on the barrel of the rifle, rolled his shoulders, and said, "Works for me."

I didn't respond.

Except to press down on the accelerator.

———

The front gates were open and I expected to be hit by a hail of gunfire as we tore up to the house, tires squealing on the pavement.

Instead...there was nothing.

Nothing as we screeched to a stop, as we got out of the car a shit-ton more quietly.

Carter and I exchanged glances, nods, gestures, and then I was moving quickly up to the front door, standing to the side of it, reaching for the handle.

It moved, and with another quick glance back at Carter, who was covering me, I stepped inside.

Knowing he'd be right behind me.

The entry was grand and huge and...dead.

Quiet. Furniture covered with sheets. Dust on the floor.

Footprints leading down the hall.

Carter paused behind me, clearly noted the same. "Let's move," he muttered.

We started winding our way through the mansion, making it into another wing of the house, the floor less dusty here—more tramped through, but still with an easy enough trail to follow.

And then out of the shadows a big fucker emerged, his gun out, his eyes trained on us. "I won't miss this time."

I didn't misunderstand his implication.

He wouldn't miss...like he had last time outside of Frankie's store.

My gun was pointed right at his chest. Carter's too. "Neither will we."

I saw his intent a moment before he fired out a shot...and that was the only reason it missed us.

I dove to the ground, Carter behind me, both of us rolling to the side through a large pass-through, landing in a room with even more covered furniture.

At least we had cover.

"Go," Carter ordered, taking up position behind a couch as that big bastard stalked into the room. "I'll cover you. Ready?"

An inhale. An exhale.

"Ready," I muttered.

"Three. Two. *One.*" He popped up, started firing off shots.

The big fucker dove to the side, taking up his own cover, and then I was sprinting back out of the room, down the hall, and—

Nearly running into Frankie.

I skidded to a halt, eyes widening as I processed what she held—a lamp, its shade battered to hell and back.

"Fuck, baby," I said, grabbing her and yanking her against my side. "Are you okay?"

A long, slow blink. "Lex?"

Shit.

Shock settling in.

I moved us back, moved us through the door she'd run through, immediately clocked why she was heading for shock.

Francis Lyon was collapsed in a heap on the floor, blood dripping down his face, pooling around his head.

"I hit him," she whispered. "I hit him a lot."

Lamp meet temple.

Yeah, I was getting that.

"Stay here, baby," I ordered gently, and then I moved toward Francis, rolled him to his back, and slapped on a pair of handcuffs.

For the second time in as many months.

I couldn't lie—it felt fucking great.

Especially as Attie ran into the room, Carter a second behind her. Ats was pissed. Carter barely had a hair out of place.

"Good?" I asked him.

A slow smile. "Not even a problem."

"The team has secured the other room and is locking down the rest of the house." A glare at Carter, at me. "You're both fucking stupid."

"Yell at me later," I muttered. "I need to get Frankie out of here."

Her mouth opened. Closed.

Then she glanced at Frankie, back to me. Nodded.

She'd save her yelling for later.

Good enough.

"Let's move," she ordered.

Sandwiching Frankie, we made our way out of the mansion and to my car.

I jumped in the back with her in my arms.

Carter got us back to Darlington.

I got her to my apartment.

Debriefs could wait.

Statements could fuck off.

Right now, I had the woman I loved in my arms, and she was safe and unharmed and the biggest risk to her had just given us enough to make sure he stayed locked up for the rest of his life.

Drugs.

People.

Kidnapping.

"Lex?"

I glanced down, realized I'd stopped with her in my arms, was standing in the middle of my kitchen, wanting to turn around and go murder Francis Lyon.

But since that would end up with me locked away from Frankie, I tabled the urge.

"Yeah, baby?"

"Will you put me down?"

My heart convulsed, but I nodded, set her on her feet. "You okay?"

A deep breath, her shoulders rising and falling, and then she said something I didn't expect. "I did it."

I frowned, moved closer, cupping her jaw in one hand. "What's that, baby?"

"I did it," she whispered. "I stood up to him. I fought for myself. I didn't slink away and hope that he didn't care enough to follow. I showed him." Her eyes came to mine. "I showed him exactly how strong I was."

"Considering I still have the lamp in the back of my car, I can agree with that, tigress."

She blinked—once, twice.

Then she smiled. "I really fucking hated that lamp."

My mouth curved. "And you certainly showed it who's boss." Her father too.

Her smile widened. Then she was up on tiptoe, her arms around my neck. "I think we need to..."

I expected her to say we needed to celebrate by breaking in my bed or the kitchen counter or my shower.

She didn't.

Her next words weren't nearly as good as that.

But they were still pretty fucking great.

"...give a statement to the FBI."

EPILOGUE

I was getting married in fifteen minutes.

To a man who was my every fantasy.

So, it was an understatement and a half that I didn't want to find a note on the counter of Earthly Delights that had a familiar flower on it.

A flower I hadn't seen since the events that had led to my facing off with my father, with him ending up in federal prison.

The trial was starting in a few weeks—his lawyers expensive and skilled and doing everything they could to delay the process.

But it was pretty much a done deal.

The charges meant he would be in prison for the rest of his life.

And Lex's discovery the night he'd kidnapped me meant they'd had the information to seriously dismantle my father's operations—something that had apparently begun with the defection of my brothers from the family business and a serious competitor cropping up here in the States.

Drugs and people were still being traded—and unfortunately probably always would be—but the Lyons were out of the business.

Or were supposed to be.

A breath as I braced myself for what I would find inside the letter.

Then...

I decided that I didn't need to brace.

That I didn't need to read it at all.

It was my wedding day.

It was my future.

I'd faced my past, moved on, built something different.

I didn't need to look back.

So, I breathed again, closed my eyes and took in my home, my happiness, the scent of my shop, the familiar noises.

Then I tossed the note into the trash.

As I straightened, I saw the basket of bows next to the register.

Bows that Lex had helped me tie in front of a crappy TV show he pretended to hate.

My eyes moved to the table with my specialty baked goods—which now consisted of six different varieties.

Then to the shelves and the window displays and the hallway that led to the kitchen.

Then to the bell as it rang over the door.

And the love of my life walked in.

He skidded to a stop just inside Earthly Delights, but only for a moment.

Because then he was walking toward me, cupping my cheeks in his big, warm palms. "You are fucking *beautiful*, baby."

My heart skittered. My belly went all squishy.

I grinned up at him. "You look really hot in a suit."

He froze.

Then he was grinning too.

Then he was kissing me, probably messing up my lipstick, *definitely* messing up my hair.

Newsflash, I didn't care.

Because this was my love, my life, my future.

He broke the kiss, smiled down at me. "You ready for this, tigress?"

I traced that beautiful curve of his lips.

"I'm ready for anything as long as it's with you."

ATTIE

I watched my partner smile down at the woman he loved and knew that I would never have that.

Not because I thought I didn't deserve it—which I didn't.

Not because I had some heavy past drama that would make me unable to open up—which I did.

Not even because I was married to my job—which I was.

But because I'd just watched the only person I'd ever thought might be the one for me get married to the love of his life.

And I fucking loved her too.

She was beautiful, sweet, and perfect for him.

I wasn't.

I—

"Kills, doesn't it?"

I jumped—which really did some damage to my street cred, if I was being honest—and turned to see Cam leaning against the building.

"Jesus, Cam," I muttered, shaking my head before I started to move by him.

He caught my arm, turned me back to face him, "I asked you a question."

My heart started pounding, but I ignored it. "Actually, you grunted three words at me." I tugged at my arm.

His fingers tightened and he crouched a little to meet my eyes. "Ats, honey. It will get better."

Now my heart had surpassed pounding.

It was lurching against my ribs, throwing itself against my bones, trying desperately to escape the confines of my chest. "I'm fine."

I was always fine.

Always.

I tugged at my arm again.

"You're not fine," he said. "You're slowly dying inside."

I was. God, help me, I *was.*

"How do you know?" I whispered.

Then immediately wanted to rip the words from the air and shove them back into my mouth.

Especially, when I chanced meeting his eyes again—and saw how gentle they were.

My throat tightened.

My eyes—God, help me—went damp.

I tugged my arm again, hard enough that I managed to free myself for a second.

And only a second.

Because then Cam was grabbing my arm again. Only, he didn't stop there. He drew me against his chest, wrapped his arms tightly around me.

And...he hugged me.

My lungs hitched.

Tears were imminent.

Fuck. That couldn't happen.

I ripped myself out of his hold, turned, took one step—

And found myself in Cam's arms again. "Don't, Ats," he began. "It's okay—"

It wasn't okay. It was very *not* okay.

Because that was the moment panic took over, my brain shut down...

I rose on tiptoe.

And...I slanted my mouth over his.

———

Thank you for reading! I hope you enjoyed Lex and Frankie as much as I loved writing their journey! Cam—our final Jackson brother—is going to get his HEA in KNOTTED LACES. **What happens when I fall for the woman who's in love with my brother?**

CLICK HERE TO READ KNOTTED LACES NOW>

———

And don't miss LACE 'EM UP from the Bang Brothers Hockey series.

Meet the Bang Brothers—five hot hockey-playing brothers who are allergic to commitment.

The brothers are about to face off against their newly-retired mother...who suddenly has plenty of time to play matchmaker. Add in their baby sister and some secret dating, a single dad, an accidental pregnancy, a marriage of convenience, and a wrong bed—or two—and these siblings are not going to know what hit them!

CLICK HERE TO READ LACE 'EM UP NOW>

———

And if you enjoyed LOST CAUSE, you'll love the sexy, sweet, and close-knit Breakers Hockey crew. The first book in the series, BROKEN, is now live!

It is sexy, hot, adorable and such a fun read. You will not be able to put this down!" —Amazon Reviewer

———

I so appreciate your help in spreading the word about my books, including sharing with friends! Please leave a review on your favorite book site!

You can also join my Facebook group, the Fabinators, for exclusive giveaways and sneak peeks of future books.

If you'd like to receive emails from me for new releases and monthly giveaway sign up for my newsletter at https://www.elisefaber.com/newsletter

LIFE SUCKS SERIES

Life Sucks Series
Train Wreck
Hot Mess
Dumpster Fire
Clusterf*@k
FUBAR
Perfect Storm
Free Fall
Lost Cause

ALSO BY ELISE FABER

Billionaire's Club (all stand alone)

Bad Night Stand

Bad Breakup

Bad Husband

Bad Hookup

Bad Divorce

Bad Fiancé

Bad Boyfriend

Bad Blind Date

Bad Wedding

Bad Engagement

Bad Bridesmaid

Bad Swipe

Bad Girlfriend

Bad Best Friend

Bad Rebound

Bad Romance

Bad Business

Bad Billionaire's Quickies

Sinful Bosses (all stand alone)

Ruthless Billionaire

Gold Hockey (all stand alone)

Blocked

Backhand

Boarding

Benched

Breakaway

Breakout

Checked

Coasting

Centered

Charging

Caged

Crashed

A Gold Christmas

Cycled

Caught

Cap

Covered

Crushed

Changed

Scored

Breakers Hockey (all stand alone)

Broken

Boldly

Breathless

Ballsy

Bewitched

Blowout

Breathe

Blazed

Sierra Hockey Series

Over the Line

The Big Skate

Caught from Behind

On the Fly

Rush Hockey Trilogy #1

Big Puck Energy

Filthy Puckboy

So Pucking Over It

Rush Hockey Trilogy #2

Love, Pucks, and Other Stories

All's Fair in Pucks and War

No Pucks Lost Between Us

Eagles Hockey Series (all stand alone)

Broken Laces

Knotted Laces

Lace 'em Up

Love, Action, Camera (all stand alone)

Dotted Line

Action Shot

Close-Up

End Scene

Meet Cute

Love After Midnight (all stand alone)

Rum And Notes

Virgin Daiquiri

On The Rocks

Sex On The Seats

Life Sucks Series

Train Wreck

Hot Mess

Dumpster Fire

Clusterf*@k

FUBAR

Perfect Storm

Free Fall

Lost Cause

Roosevelt Ranch Series (all stand alone, series complete)

Disaster at Roosevelt Ranch

Heartbreak at Roosevelt Ranch

Collision at Roosevelt Ranch

Regret at Roosevelt Ranch

Desire at Roosevelt Ranch

Phoenix Series (read in order)

Phoenix Rising

Dark Phoenix

Phoenix Freed

Phoenix: LexTal Chronicles (rereleasing soon, stand alone, Phoenix world)

From Ashes

In Flames

To Smoke

KTS Series (all stand alone, series complete)

Riding The Edge

Crossing The Line

Leveling The Field

Scorching The Earth

Cocky Heroes World

Tattooed Troublemaker

About the Author

USA Today bestselling author, Elise Faber, loves chocolate, Star Wars, Harry Potter, and hockey (the order depending on the day and how well her team -- the Sharks! -- are playing). She and her husband also play as much hockey as they can squeeze into their schedules, so much so that their typical date night is spent on the ice. Elise is the mom to two exuberant boys and lives in Northern California. Connect with her in her Facebook group, the Fabinators or find more information about her books at www.elisefaber.com.

📘 facebook.com/elisefaberauthor

ⓐ amazon.com/author/elisefaber

BB bookbub.com/profile/elise-faber

📷 instagram.com/elisefaber

♪ tiktok.com/@elisefaberauthor

g goodreads.com/elisefaber